S0-EGF-012

Amanda was afraid to move…

They put on their coats and headed for the door. As Dieter switched off the lights, a single spotlight turned on in the catwalk gallery.

"There's no one there. That light must be on a timer," Dieter said.

They walked up the staircase leading to the catwalk. With each step, Amanda's anxiety grew. They passed half a dozen small paintings by Kruger. Finally, they came to the spotlighted work. It was as if the mugger's hand had again covered Amanda's nose and mouth. A silent scream clawed the inside of her throat. The canvas was about seventy-five by ninety centimeters and framed in black-lacquered wood. The brush strokes were bold but well defined. The vibrant colors had a painfully vivid quality, a style reminiscent of the American painter Edward Hopper.

Depicted in grim detail was Marlene, just as Amanda had found her: long blonde hair draped across the rim of the bathtub, the stab wounds, the crimson water, the whole horrific scene.

A luscious mélange of art, love, and murder…

In Cologne, West Germany, in the 1980s, Amanda Lee, a young American gallery owner, discovered the murdered body of her business partner, Marlene Eichler. Hours later, she found a painting that depicted the scene down to the jagged knife wounds and splattered blood. She offered to help the police identify the artist/killer, but learned that she was a prime suspect, along with her partner's ex-husband. Thrown together by circumstance, she found herself falling deeply in love with him, even though her senses screamed beware. She soon realized how little she knew about Marlene as she waded through the murky waters of her past—illicit affairs, a tumultuous marriage, and underworld connections. Now Amanda had to confront the mind-numbing truth and the terror of a brutal demise as she stumbled across her own death painting.

KUDOS for *When Death Imitates Art*

In *When Death Imitates Art* by P. D. Halt, Amanda Lee is an art gallery owner in Cologne, Germany, in the 1980s, along with her business partner, Marlene Eichler. One night Amanda is mugged in front of the gallery, and then released from the hospital into Marlene's care, going to Marlene's home to spend the night convalescing. However, much to her dismay, the next morning, Amanda finds Marlene murdered in an upstairs bathroom, while Amanda slept on the couch. The police suspect Amanda, along with Marlene's ex-husband, but, other than that, they don't seem to really care who killed her. Then a painting of Marlene's death scene shows up at the gallery. Amanda is frightened, but she's determined to find the real killer—if she survives the investigation. Well written, fast paced, and intriguing, the story pulls you in from the very first page and holds your interest all the way through to the startling conclusion. A really great read. ~ *Taylor Jones, The Review Team of Taylor Jones & Regan Murphy*

When Death Imitates Art by P. D. Halt is the story of a young American who finds herself stranded in Germany but manages to make the best of it. When Amanda Lee moved to Cologne, Germany, in the 1980s, she was expecting to get married. But her fiancé, Karl, who professed his undying love in New York, had a change of heart once they got to Germany, breaking the engagement and shattering her heart. Rather than go back to New York to face her skeptical friends, Amanda decides to go into business with a German friend, Marlene Eichler, and start up an art gallery. Things go very well for the two until Amanda gets mugged and then, later, finds Marlene murdered at her home where Amanda has been convalescing. To make things worse, the police suspect Amanda. Convinced that the police are not really looking for the killer, and instead, are trying to blame it on her, she decides to investigate on her own, unwittingly painting a target on herself. *When Death Imitates Art* is well written and hard to put down. Halt's character development is superb, and her vivid scene descriptions make you feel like you're there. The surprise ending will stump even the most die-hard mystery fans. If you like hard-to-solve mysteries, you're going to love this one. ~ *Regan Murphy, The Review Team of Taylor Jones & Regan*

ACKNOWLEDGMENTS

I would like to thank Mystery Writers of America, New York Chapter, for its strong support and outstanding programs. Nancy Hughes, Daniella Bernett, and former chapter president, Richie Narvaez, were especially helpful. I'm grateful to the hard-working people at Black Opal Books, who brought this project to light; to Robert Kenney, of Thoughtful Editing, for his patience and invaluable contributions; and to Friedhelm and Cristina Kleinau, of Düsseldorf and Hamburg, for their encouragement and help from the very beginning.

A special thanks to my best friend, Diane Seidle, who has always been my partner in crime, be it shopping for shoes or literary pursuits. When it came to this book, she jumped right in, using her considerable artistic and marketing talents on my behalf, with hours of hard work. I must also give a shout-out to her patient husband, Ivan, for being okay with it all.

Note: In Germany, women over a certain age are referred to as *Frau,* whether or not they are married.

WHEN DEATH IMITATES ART

P. D. HALT

A Black Opal Books Publication

GENRE: MYSTERY-DETECTIVE/WOMEN SLEUTHS/THRILLER

This is a work of fiction. Names, places, characters and incidents are either the product of the author's imagination or are used fictitiously, and any resemblance to any actual persons, living or dead, businesses, organizations, events, or locales is entirely coincidental. All trademarks, service marks, registered trademarks, and registered service marks are the property of their respective owners and are used herein for identification purposes only. The publisher does not have any control over or assume any responsibility for author or third-party websites or their contents.

DEDICATION

In loving memory of James Sullivan,
who never stopped believing in me.

PROLOGUE

Cologne, West Germany, 1960:

L ike apparitions in the night, shadows of the small film crew moved silently into position as the camera began to roll. On cue, her robe cascaded to the floor, becoming a silk pool around her feet and leaving her naked and helpless, blinking in the glare of the kliegs. She grabbed the artist's hand, bowed her head, and followed him to a vat filled to the brim with red paint. Hesitating only for a moment, she allowed herself to be submerged. A nearby canvas, gleaming white against the darkness, stood ready to consume the imprint of her breasts and abdomen, the essence of her youth and beauty.

She walked back to the vat and was dipped once more, like angel cake into a strawberry sauce, to be pressed into a second canvas, this time echoing her contours from her face to the graceful line of her thighs. This process was repeated over and over.

Still adorned in nothing but paint, the scarlet muse smiled and posed next to the artist in front of some two dozen works.

Suddenly, she grabbed her throat. The camera moved in for a close up. Her lips quivered, and her eyes grew wide with fear. She resembled a swimmer trapped in an undertow, battling against a crushing tide. For a few moments, she struggled for air—nostrils dilating, chest heaving—then fell to the floor in a fit of involuntary shuddering that became less and less intense. Her head rolled to one side. She lay completely still.

CHAPTER 1

Cologne, West Germany, Late October 1980:

T his footage of Jürgen Ept and his model was shot twenty years ago," Dieter Becker told his television audience.

Germany's foremost art critic had a voice like a Shakespearean actor. His commanding presence made him appear to be more attractive than he was. He strode over to one of the canvases just shown in the film.

"Ept was an innovator, the first and last artist ever to experiment in this way with paints containing lead, cadmium, and chromium. Cadmium inhalation alone can kill you. To be immersed in it, well…" Dieter shook his head and lowered his voice for effect. "One can only speculate as to whether or not Ept realized this, sacrificing his model for his art. He disappeared after that. Some say he left the country. Others believe he has disguised his looks and is still painting under an assumed name right here in Cologne. In any case, these works are highly prized by collectors and bring a fortune on today's market. Strange isn't it, how death increases the value of art."

Strains of a Bach "Brandenburg Concerto" rose in the background, signifying the end of Dieter's show. Now only his face dominated the television screen.

"Before I say goodnight, I want to remind you that the Klaus Kruger exhibition at the Lee Eichler Gallery is open to the public beginning November eighth. If I were you, I wouldn't miss it. I predict that Kruger will be viewed as a modern master of the eighties. Till the same time next time, this is Dieter Becker, speaking of art."

Amanda Lee pushed the remote's *off* button, and Dieter's face disappeared in a flash of light. "That poor girl couldn't have been more than sixteen years old. Where does Dieter get this kind of thing?"

"His connections, *liebling*," Marlene Eichler said. "The TV show itself and, of course, his column in *Die Welt* put him in touch with all sorts of people." She leaned back on the office sofa as if posing for *Vogue.* Most women would have sold their souls just for her cheekbones. "Dieter mentioned our Kruger opening as he promised. That should insure a good turnout."

"Whatever Dieter claims is art, sells," Amanda said, "regardless of its merit."

"You are questioning Kruger's value as an artist?"

"Well, I personally don't like his work, but if Dieter wants us to push this man, we more or less have to."

"Without Dieter, we could not have opened this gallery," Marlene said. "And this association has not exactly hurt our sales. I would like a glass of champagne."

"What's the occasion?"

"It is Thursday, *liebling*. Isn't that occasion enough? Hans gave me a bottle of Dom Pérignon." She got up, removed the wine from the fridge, and poured it into Baccarat crystal glasses.

"It must've cost him a couple hundred marks," Amanda said.

"He can afford it."

When she and Marlene had opened their gallery the year before, they bought the best they could afford, in order to impress clients. Marlene insisted on doing their office all in white. "It is the only background for paintings and for people."

Splashes of color came from the ever-present vase of fresh flowers and from four abstracts by Günter Grah, a friend of Dieter's.

Marlene raised her glass. "To the Lee Eichler Gallery. May it make us lots of beautiful money."

Amanda could feel Marlene scrutinizing her face, her hair, and her sweater and jeans. At thirty, she still preferred minimal makeup and wore only a little baby-pink lipstick. Her hair was wash and wear, held back with a clip.

"Why do you wear these boy's clothes? You should make the most of your assets, *liebling.* If not for yourself, then for the sake of our business."

"In the States, we call them classics, and how I look doesn't affect the gallery. I haven't heard any complaints about the way I handle the finances or mount our shows."

"You work hard. I would not say otherwise. It is just that, if you fixed yourself up a little, you could participate more in client meetings and parties, get to know the people who can help us," Marlene said.

"That's your job, and you're so much better at it than I am," Amanda said. "My German is still sketchy. Besides, I prefer to concentrate on the art end of things."

"For your own good, you must be able to handle any part of the business. What if something happened to me?"

"I've never seen you in better health."

"The pressure of the Kruger reception is starting to weigh on me." Marlene stretched like some exotic feline. "It will be the biggest party we have ever given and the most expensive. Dieter has invited dozens of prominent collectors. He is even videotaping our festivities for his television show. This time, I cannot handle it all by myself. I need you to be there to help and to look the part of a successful gallery owner."

Amanda stared down at her shoes. They had seen better days. None of Dieter's friends would buy a postcard from someone who looked like this, much less a painting. Even her "good clothes" were dated. Reluctantly, she began to see her friend's point. "Okay, I'll try."

Marlene's expression went from petulant to gleeful. "Wonderful." She glanced at her watch. "Let me see if my hairdresser can fit you in."

"Now? Can't it wait a few days?"

"Now is always the best time." Marlene picked up the phone and began to dial. "Then we will go shopping for clothes, yes?" Her blue eyes danced with the prospect of the makeover. "It will be fun, *liebling*. You will see."

Half an hour later, they arrived at the posh salon of Ute Bauer and entered a soothing world of crystal sconces, antique mirrors, and aqua silk. A combination of hair and beauty preparations scented the air. While Marlene looked on, Ute combed Amanda's hair, pulling it back, parting it in different places, studying the length and texture.

"What if we lighten it a little?" Marlene said.

"What's wrong with brown?"

"You will make an irresistible blonde."

Ute brought out a chart of glamorous possibilities from platinum to dark ash. Marlene selected a shade very like her own, and Ute applied the color. Next came the cut. "Do a smooth bob that just brushes the shoulders," Marlene said.

"Do we have to cut it? Couldn't we just—"

"No!"

When the makeup artist began, Marlene worked with

him. "Use the ivory foundation. Like me, she is fair. Pay attention," Marlene said to Amanda. "You must learn to do this for yourself."

With every stroke of a sponge, brush, or pencil, Amanda's "potential" became reality. She couldn't get over the change. She found the transformation unnerving, but exciting.

"See. Are you not stunning?" Marlene said. They left the salon with a chic tote stuffed with cosmetics. "Now we will see what Sophia has for us," Marlene said, as they headed for the Trella Boutique.

Sofia Danielle, a slender Italian in her late forties, welcomed them at the door. "Frau Lee, so nice to meet you at last. Frau Eichler has told me so much about you. As you probably know, she buys most of her clothes from me. You look to be the same size." Sophia took out a tape measure and confirmed her assessment. After disappearing into the back for a few minutes, she returned with an armload of clothes and placed them in a large dressing room. It reminded Amanda of playing dress-up as a little girl.

"Clothes are wonderful attitude changers," Marlene said. "What you wear affects how you feel and how others feel about you."

"I don't think I can afford all this," Amanda whispered. "Unlike you, I don't have a rich ex-husband sending me checks every month."

"Nonsense. We will sell lots and lots of Kruger

paintings," she whispered back. "Think of it as an investment."

Sophia carefully wrapped a Jil Sander suit, a French angora dress with matching Maude Frizon shoes, and several pairs of leather pants with matching cashmere sweaters.

"If, from time to time you see something special for her," Marlene said to Sophia, "send it over on approval."

"Don't you think this is enough?" Amanda asked.

"No, *liebling*. We have but one life. We should enjoy it, yes?"

Loaded down with white packages tied in black ribbons, they made their way along the cobbled street, now crowded with people hurrying home. An attractive man turned to stare at them.

"He has never seen two such beauties before," Marlene said.

"Do you know him?"

"Unfortunately, no."

"He probably has a wife and ten kids."

The sun was sinking fast, streaking the November sky with antique gold. The bells of Kölner Dom serenaded the chilly air, and shops began to close with the usual German punctuality. The two women joked and laughed like schoolgirls all the way back to the gallery. As they came through the front door, Marlene's direct line lit up.

"Marlene Eichler here."

Amanda watched in surprise as Marlene grew pale

and began to tremble. Without a word, she hung up.

"What's the matter? Who was that?"

"Nobody, *liebling*. A wrong number, that is all."

"But you look so strange. Are you sure?"

"I am sure." Marlene grabbed her purse. "I must get ready for dinner with Hans Demuth. Tonight, I close the sale on the Cristopin I showed him. You should leave too. It is almost six o'clock."

"Rolf's coming at six-thirty to help me mount the Kruger show, remember?"

"Don't stay too late. When you leave, let Rolf see you to your car." Marlene blew a kiss over her shoulder and hurried out the door.

Busy lining up paintings against the wall, Amanda didn't hear their young assistant, Rolf Röhr, come in. "I thought I was working with Frau Lee tonight," he said.

"You are." Amanda put down a canvas and turned around.

"My God. From just a few meters away, you look exactly like Frau Eichler."

*ဗာ*ဗာ

Blood spurted from a butterfly with a five-foot wing-span. It lay crumpled and broken across a Klaus Kruger canvas. "If this is art," Rolf said, "I prefer the stains on my T-shirt."

"I'm not crazy about Kruger either," Amanda said,

"but Dieter Becker calls him the *Neue Sachlichkeit* artist of the eighties."

"Sounds like another one of Herr Becker's marketing ploys."

"Maybe so, but as Marlene likes to remind me, Dieter's choices sell whether I agree with them or not, even New Objectivity revivalism."

Rolf hoisted the monumental work into place and adjusted the spotlight above it. "How's this?"

"Perfect," she said. "That's the last one."

He climbed down from the ladder and took a swallow of warm Coke. "You really look different. I can't get over the change. You looked nice before, but now…"

"Thank you."

He gave her a boyish grin and pushed a lock of dark hair from his eyes. "Is that it for tonight?"

"Yes, thank God." She looked at her watch. Midnight. "I didn't realize it was so late."

"Do you want me to wait for you? Cologne is not as safe as it used to be."

"I'll be okay. I lived in New York, remember?"

"Well then, I'll be going. See you tomorrow." He pulled on his leather jacket and went out into the night. A few moments later, Rolf roared off on his motorcycle. Through the glass door, Amanda watched the taillight dwindle until it disappeared. She was tired but content.

What was that? She thought she saw something move in the shadows outside to the left. After a few seconds, she decided it was just a shrub tossed by the wind.

She walked back into the gallery's exhibition space and surveyed the night's work. The canvases were arranged for dramatic effect and loomed over a polished floor of one thousand square feet. The interior of the place was spare but elegant, reflecting the Bauhaus influence. On three sides, windows started at the twenty-foot ceiling and came down about a quarter of the way to let in an abundance of natural light. Beneath them, the larger paintings were exhibited. On the back wall, a catwalk gallery displayed smaller works. A spiral staircase graced one end. Kruger's work filled both the main and catwalk galleries. A single acid-green *K*, his signature, was a key element in each composition. Professing a belief that death was the ultimate experience, he made it the subject of his work. What did Dieter see in him?

On one canvas, a pack of wolves menaced a rabbit. The tiny creature's eyes were filled with terror as it awaited its fate. In another work, a young woman hung from the end of a rope, her face contorted in agony. Amanda turned off the spots. A lurid light drifted in from the windows, giving the macabre visions a ghostly quality that all but chased her from the room.

She collapsed into her office chair and started to tackle the stack of RSVPs on her desk. The collectors' reception was just over a week from now. The phone rang, shattering the quiet. Who could that be at this hour? "Lee Eichler Gallery." Aberrant sound was the response.

After a few moments, it ended with a click. A spidery chill crept up Amanda's back. *Probably just a wrong number*, she told herself. *Could it be the same "wrong number" that had upset Marlene earlier? The RSVPs can wait. It's time to leave, the sooner, the better.*

Outside, the wind had picked up, causing the trees to sway like drunken dancers. She hurried to her old VW and unlocked the door.

She heard erratic breathing directly behind her. Before she could turn around a gloved hand covered her nose and mouth, jerking her head backward. Within seconds, she was suffocating.

CHAPTER 2

Panic overtook rational thought as Amanda pushed and kicked, trying to wrench away from her attacker. She managed to bite him hard on the finger, and he released his grip. For a moment, he shook his wounded hand, and she drank in great gulps of cold air. Sharp pain surged through her chest, and a sound thinner than a whimper escaped her lips, "Help, help, anyone, please."

She tried to run on legs like Jell-O, but he latched onto her wrist, twisting it almost to the breaking point. He slammed her against the VW with such force she thought her neck might snap, then he grabbed her throat, restricting her airway once more.

Eyes stinging with tears, she tried to wriggle free. He let go, and she struggled to inhale.

"What do you want?" she managed to whisper.

"Here's my purse, there's over two hundred marks inside. Take the car too. It's worth something."

He slapped the keys out of her hand and pulled off her shoulder bag, tossing it to the ground.

"Why are you doing this?" She frantically scanned the street. Populated only by deserted shops and galleries, she saw no hope for rescue. There wasn't a soul in sight, except the creature in front of her reeking of rage and alcohol. He seized a fistful of hair and forced her to look into his eyes. Ice blue, they glared from behind a ski mask.

"Stop!"

His hand went up, and she saw the glint of steel. She reached for the mask, and he hit her with such intensity, she fell crashing onto the cobblestones.

❧❧❧

The ruby-red Porsche rumbled into the parking lot of the Klimt Cafe. Marlene turned off the ignition and checked herself in the mirror.

At thirty-eight, fine lines were beginning to form around her eyes and mouth, but she still looked good.

Luckily, she had inherited her mother's bone structure. That was all her mother had given her except for an old photo and a thin volume of poems. At age six, Marlene had been left to the mercy of a state-run orphanage. "I will be back for you, *liebling*," her mother had said.

Only she never came back. At first, little Marlene would wait every Sunday in a large room with the other postwar *kinder* who hoped to be reunited with relatives or to be adopted. She would wait for her mother long after the room was empty. Eventually, she no longer expected her mother to come.

She freshened her lipstick. Tonight at dinner, she would complete the sale of a painting worth DM 10,000 to Hans Demuth, then she would not see him anymore. He was a whiner and a bore. Had she not been so lonely the night she met Hans, she would never have bothered with him. Now he acted as if he owned her. What a turnoff. She had already moved on to someone else whose slightly dangerous aura was much more sexually exciting. She couldn't wait to see him later that evening.

A valet opened the car door. His youthful face reflected lust and admiration as she exited the car one shapely leg at a time.

As usual, the Klimt offered up a cheerful mixture of music, laughter, and conversation. She lifted her chin, and the hood of her black cashmere coat slid down around her shoulders, revealing a tumble of silky hair.

Pilger, the owner, took her coat. "Good evening, Frau Eichler. Herr Demuth is waiting for you over there," he said, indicating a trim, attractive young man in his early thirties.

Demuth touched a napkin to his mustache and stood up, watching them approach.

"*Lieber* Hans, what are you doing way over here sitting in the dark? Herr Pilger, please find us another table, well located, near the window perhaps."

"But, Marlene, I do not want to be seen," Demuth hissed. "I have taken risks enough just coming to a place like this. What if Helga or any of her friends…"

"I did not wear my new Chanel to stay hidden in a corner. Besides, Hans, if anyone sees us, we are discussing a painting you wish to buy. A present for Helga, yes?"

Reluctantly, he followed Marlene and Herr Pilger through the middle of the crowded restaurant to a prime table. Several people stared in their direction, especially the men at the bar. Marlene, well aware that the black slip of a dress clung to every curve, smiled back at them. She waved to some friends across the restaurant. "Brigette, Reiner, *hallo*."

"Marlene, please. Why do you do this? If Helga finds out about you, she'll throw me out and leave me penniless."

"Hans, I told you before, Marlene is not a toy you play with in secret. Herr Pilger, a bottle of Champagne Krug, please."

In spite of the fact that he deserved it, Marlene felt little triumph in making Hans squirm. She barely listened as he went on about how dull his marriage had become. She had heard it all before, too many times. Instead, her thoughts wandered to Wolf Eichler, her ex-husband.

What a contrast. She would always regret losing him. Wolf had made her feel truly loved for the first time in her life. A million trifles like Hans or even her new conquest would never make up for that.

The waiter arrived at the table and opened the champagne with a festive pop. "What do you expect me to do?" Hans said as he finished his lament.

She took the first glass—the bubbles tickled her nose. "I expect you to try this excellent wine."

"Seriously, Marlene. You know how much I love you. No other woman has ever gotten to me the way you have. I think of you every moment."

"Of course, Hans," she said. "By the way, did you bring the money for the painting? I must have it tonight." Under the table, he moved his hand along her leg. How predictable. She smiled and brushed it away. Hans reached into his inside pocket and took out an envelope.

"It contains ten one-thousand-mark notes."

"Thank you." She plucked the envelope from his hand and shoved it into her small Chanel bag. "I do not want to stay for dinner."

Hans brightened. "I will just take care of the bill, and we can leave at once. I can hardly wait to—"

"I am leaving alone." Marlene got up from the table. "I think it best if we do not see each other again."

"*What?*"

"Shhhh. Do not create a scene. Helga, remember? Your painting will be delivered tomorrow." She walked toward the door without looking back.

এ৯৫৯

The wail of the siren fell mute as the police car skidded to a halt. Green and white flashing lights sent layers of shadows flying across the rain-washed architecture of the Pfeilstrasse. "The report said a woman had been attacked in front of this gallery." The young officer left the vehicle and searched the area with his flashlight. "Nothing here but an old VW."

"Come on. We were off duty five minutes ago," his partner said, starting the engine.

As he turned to go back, the policeman spotted something on the ground behind the Volkswagen. He shone his light in that direction revealing the body of a young woman, her skin and hair glistening in the rain. A stream of blood flowed from a gash above her left temple and ran in rivulets between the cobblestones. He heard a moan. "Call an ambulance!" he shouted.

CHAPTER 3

Amanda drifted up from a bottomless sea and felt a wave of consciousness break over her. For a moment, she couldn't remember what had happened. She lay in a hospital bed with an IV needle taped into place on her right arm. With her free hand, she felt a thick bandage on the side of her head, and memories of the attack began to return. Her body ached, and her throat felt like parchment. Slowly, she became aware of a persistent rattling and turned her head in the direction of the noise. Sitting in a chair near the bed and flipping through the current issue of *Paris Vogue* was Marlene.

A taupe suit skimmed her figure, the skirt split in just the right place to show plenty of leg. She paused for a moment to push an errant strand of hair out of her eyes and resumed perusing the magazine.

Amanda might have known she'd be there. She always seemed to turn up in an emergency. They'd first met at the post office, where Amanda tried, in newly learned German, to convince a resolute clerk to give her a package from New York even though she'd misplaced the notice. A long and angry line had formed behind her. Marlene stepped out of the line and came to her rescue. She turned on an irresistible charm that swept away all opposition.

"For that, you deserve the drink of your choice. This package contains my wedding dress," Amanda said. That was how their friendship began.

Amanda's wedding didn't happen. The undying love Karl professed in New York seemed to evaporate when they arrived in Germany. This, after she had given up her job at the Lace Gallery, her apartment in lower Manhattan, and her life there. She had taken such an emotional bludgeoning, the last thing she needed was to go back and face all the "I told you so's." She decided to stay on in Europe, at least for a while.

About the same time, Marlene's husband, Wolf Eichler, sued for divorce. The two new friends spent hours cheering each other up. They discovered that they both loved and collected art. This gave birth to the idea for the gallery. Chances for success seemed good since Cologne was the center for European contemporary art.

"*Liebling,* you are awake finally! You gave me such a scare." Marlene, her eyes filled with concern, came to the side of the bed to give Amanda a hug.

"Well," Amanda said, touching her bandage, "there's at least one person in town who doesn't like my new look."

"I am so glad you are all right. The police called me after finding our business card in your wallet; the money was gone. They said that you had been mugged, but you could not identify the man."

"I talked to the police?"

"Apparently. In the ambulance on the way to the hospital."

"I don't remember."

Marlene sat on the edge of the bed. "After what you have been through, I am not surprised."

"How did they find me?"

"An anonymous caller. Had the police not arrived when they did, you would have bled to death."

"This caller must have seen everything."

"The police have no way of finding him. They are treating your case as an ordinary mugging. I doubt they will give it much attention."

"If they don't catch this guy, he'll be free to do it again."

"Do not distress yourself," Marlene said. "You need to rest."

"He was so intense, so brutal. I've never seen such hatred in anyone's eyes. He looked as if he wanted to kill me, but I don't know why."

℘℘℘

It was Saturday. Amanda was feeling better and longed to leave the hospital. Neurological tests were negative, and there appeared to be no permanent damage. At six-thirty p.m., Marlene walked through the door with the doctor.

"*Liebling*, you look so much better today."

"I'm feeling better."

Dr. Braun, a neat little man with a precise manner, examined her stitches and replaced the large bandage with a small flesh-colored one. "You are healing nicely and will not have a scar," he said. "However, since you have suffered a head injury, I must insist on complete rest for at least a week." He turned to Marlene, who was staring out the window at the street below. "Frau Eichler—"

Marlene jumped at the sound of her name. "Yes?"

"—she can leave with you now if you promise to bring her back here immediately should any problem occur."

"Yes, yes, of course, Herr Doctor."

"That's wonderful," Amanda said. "I thought I'd have to stay at least until tomorrow." She started to get up, and, for a moment, the room did a slow spin.

"Not so fast, please," the doctor said.

He gave Amanda two bottles of pills: an antibiotic and something for pain. He bowed slightly and left.

Marlene shoved the door closed and opened a large tote. She pulled out a sweat suit and sneakers retrieved from Amanda's apartment. "Put these on, and we will leave at once."

"What's the matter? You're a nervous wreck. I've never seen you like this."

"I am just a little overtired. It has been a long day."

Outside, the sky was the color of lead. Amanda was surprised to see a taxi waiting at the curb instead of Marlene's Porsche. A hospital attendant wheeled her down the walkway and helped her into the back seat. "Where's your car?" Amanda asked Marlene.

"Sometimes I prefer to take a taxi."

"Since when?"

Marlene gave the driver her address on the outskirts of Cologne. Traffic was light as the taxi headed for the Konrad-Adenauer-Ufer along the Rhine. A ground fog had rolled in, making the entire city seem to levitate. The Kölner Dom seemed to rise heavenward on beams from megawatt spotlights. Neither Amanda nor Marlene spoke until the driver turned onto the Autobahn.

"What's wrong?" Amanda asked.

Marlene leaned back and closed her eyes. "Nothing a stiff drink of vodka cannot cure."

Headlights from oncoming cars moved across her face intermittently, revealing a weariness Amanda hadn't seen before. Forty minutes later, the taxi pulled into the driveway and stopped. It drove away as soon as the two women got out.

"Bastard," Marlene said. "He could have at least waited until we were inside the gate."

They stood at the entrance to a luxury complex surrounded by a high stone wall. Marlene took out an electronic key, and the tall wrought-iron gate slid open.

The complex, a restored collection of twelfth-century buildings, reflected the haunting beauty of another age. There were twelve gray stone duplexes, two and three stories tall, each facing onto a large courtyard. Rectangles of muted light, emanating from drawn curtains, were the only sign of life. Amanda realized she hadn't been there in a long time.

The silvery light of a cold moon coalesced with the golden glow of the street lamps. Marlene held onto Amanda's arm, helping her negotiate the frost-covered cobblestones. Her painkiller was wearing off; her legs felt heavy, and her head throbbed. They finally reached Marlene's two-story condo off by itself in the farthest corner of the square. A quick search of Marlene's bag produced the keys, and within moments, they stood in the warmth of the hallway. To the left were stairs leading to the master bedroom and the guest room. To the right was the living room.

Marlene helped Amanda with her coat. "You look awful," she said.

"So do you!"

They looked at each other for a moment and burst out laughing.

"What happened to the two beauties?" they both said at once.

"Go into the living room. I will take your things upstairs. I have picked up everything you will need during your stay."

Amanda switched on a small lamp and looked around. The room was quintessential Marlene. Her life-sized portrait hung over the fireplace. Posed in a tuxedo, she wore a sultry expression à la Dietrich. On either side of the carved mantle, bookcases reached from floor to ceiling, book titles obscured in this light. There were several photographs of Marlene and Wolf Eichler in polished silver frames. He'd visited the gallery right after it opened, offering congratulations, flowers, and champagne. Although he and Marlene were divorced, they seemed on good terms.

A vintage photograph of a somber young woman sat on the side table next to the lamp. Marlene's mother perhaps? Facing the outer courtyard, tall narrow windows hid behind yards of burgundy velvet. On the opposite side were French doors leading to a private walled garden. In warm weather, it was lush with all-white flowers.

Amanda collapsed on the big leather sofa placed against the back wall. She covered herself with a heavy wool throw and felt warm and relaxed for the first time in days. She must have dozed off because, all at once, Marlene was standing over her with a glass of chilled vodka. "Take this, *liebling*. It is Marlene's prescription for pain.

You will find it far more enjoyable than those awful pills."

She had bathed, washed her hair, and changed into flowing silk pajamas. Their delicate shell color illuminated her skin. Amanda raised herself to a sitting position and took the vodka.

A cheerful crackling now came from the fireplace. Curling up in a big leather chair, Marlene ran her slender fingers along the arm, almost caressing it. "This used to be Wolf's chair," she said. "We lived here such a short time, yet this room is filled with memories.

"He was so good to me, *liebling,* so warm and caring—and I threw it all away, and for what?" Her voice began to quiver. "He will never again look at me in that special way, or hold me so close I become a part of him, or brush his lips against my cheek and whisper 'I love you.' I miss him so." Marlene starred at the fire as if looking into the past. "Sometimes I hug my pillow at night, pretending it is him, then weep as I am reminded he will never be with me again. Yes, we are still on good terms, but in a way, that makes matters even worse—to have him friendly, but on such a detached level. At times when I see him, it is almost unbearable. I want to run to him, beg him to return to me, but it is too late for that now."

"Why? Maybe he feels the same way," Amanda said.

"No, I hurt him too badly, and he cannot forget it.'

"How can you be so sure, perhaps—"

"No, *liebling*, I am sure. I read it in his private journal. He does not know, but I have a key to his house in Düsseldorf. I borrowed his Mercedes once for a few hours while my car was in for servicing. The house key hung on the same ring as the car keys. I had a duplicate made. It took no time to guess the security code, zero, six, ten, seventy-nine. The day we met.

"Occasionally on his housekeeper's day off, I go there just to feel near him. I put on his robe and lie in his bed. I read the secret entries in his journal. Now he writes of me not as a desirable woman but as a child he must look after. This is how I know he does not love but pities me."

Marlene took a deep sip of vodka. The dancing flames reflected on her face, as if she were enduring the tortures of hell.

"Perhaps it's time you forget Wolf and find someone else. There are other men in your life. What about the one from Berlin you mentioned? What was his name?" Amanda said.

"At first I found him exciting but not anymore. In only a short while, his veneer of charm wore off, and his true misogynistic nature showed through. He turned out to be just another control freak who enjoys pushing women around."

"And Hans Demuth?"

Marlene leaned over the table and poured herself another drink. "A big mistake. I told him Thursday night that I no longer wished to see him. Married men are always a mistake, especially if they are supported by their wives."

"How did he take it?"

"Not well. He is a little man with a big ego," Marlene said. "He later called and actually threatened me, but he lacks the guts to do more than that."

"I'm so sorry, Marlene. You deserve much better, and I'm sure that in time the right one will come along."

Amanda knew that sounded platitudinal, but she felt it was true. Marlene was a beautiful, intelligent woman with so much to offer any man. It broke Amanda's heart to see her so depressed.

For a long time, they sat in silence, watching the fire perform its lively ballet.

"Should we be thinking about dinner?" Marlene said.

"I'm not very hungry."

"Nor I."

"Marlene, I appreciate your inviting me here to recover. At the hospital, you must have sat up most of the night waiting for me to come to."

"You are, after all, my business partner," Marlene said. "You are also the only real woman friend I have ever had, almost like a little sister. Most women are always so jealous of me there is no room for friendship. You were never like that. Liebling, what if the person who attacked you really meant to hurt me?"

"It was pretty dark. Now that I'm a blonde, it's possible someone could make that mistake. Rolf did. But why would anyone want to hurt you?"

"There are several people who are less than pleased with me. I did not want to worry you, but I have been receiving anonymous phone calls."

"Like the one on Thursday?"

"Yes. Sometimes the caller will just hang up, and sometimes they say terrible things. I thought they would eventually become bored with their little joke and stop."

"Is it a man or a woman?"

"I cannot tell. The voice is altered. It sounds almost mechanical. I had no idea this would become more than just a nuisance. I am so sorry I caused you this pain."

"We don't know for certain there's any connection. But even if there is, you had no way of knowing what would happen. I don't want you to start feeling guilty."

"There is something else. Today, while I was alone at the gallery, a package came—not a very nice surprise."

"What was it? Who sent it?"

"I will just say it was a very sick joke sent by someone evil. I do not know who." She was visibly shaken.

"Have you notified the police?"

"No. We do not need any bad publicity just before our big opening. It would not sit well with Dieter's socialite friends. We have too much money tied up in this to have it fail."

"We must call the police, regardless. You could be in real danger."

Marlene got up from her chair. "We can discuss it in the morning. Now, I think we should go up to bed."

Amanda felt the effects of the vodka on an empty stomach, and exhaustion took over. "Do you mind if I stay down here tonight? I'm just too comfortable to move, and there's enough fire to last until I fall asleep."

"Of course. Whatever you like." Marlene picked up the vodka bottle and her empty glass. "Want another?"

"No thanks."

"Very well then, goodnight, *liebling*." Marlene bent over and kissed Amanda's forehead, then went upstairs.

Amanda could sense a deep despair, an aching loneliness in Marlene. She wanted to reach out but didn't know what to say or do. Well, there was one thing she could do. She'd insist they go to the police in the morning, before something else happened. Snuggling under the wool throw, she heard the hall clock chime ten times and the telephone ring just once. Marlene must have answered it on the upstairs extension. Amanda drifted into a deep, deep sleep.

CHAPTER 4

Rain fell in sheets, and a frigid wind shook the French doors as if frantic to get in, pulling Amanda out of a murky dream. The fire had turned into charred wood and ashes. Shivering, she burrowed farther into the sofa. Her mouth felt like cotton and tasted foul. Going back to sleep wasn't an option. Wrapping the wool throw around her, she went into the front hall, looking for the thermostat. She couldn't believe Marlene had turned it all the way down. The place was freezing.

Soon the comforting sound of heat gurgled through the pipes, and she was seated at the kitchen table drinking freshly brewed coffee. It surprised her when she glanced at the clock and saw it was twelve thirty in the afternoon. She rummaged through the cabinets and refrigerator, but only found a container of yogurt and half a bottle of wine.

Heading for the guest room and a shower, Amanda paused at Marlene's room. Hearing no noise inside, she knocked. "It's getting late," she said loudly through the door. "I made some coffee, but we have to go out to eat." She moved down the hall without waiting for a reply.

The small guest room was dominated by a Biedermeier bed covered with handmade lace and oversized pillows. A delicate vase of fresh flowers bloomed on the night table and gave off a lovely scent. Amanda resisted the urge to lie down. She found her coat and one of her new sweater and pants sets hanging in the freestanding wardrobe. The big tote containing her toiletries sat on the wardrobe floor.

It felt wonderful to linger in a hot bath and turn the handheld shower on all the parts that hurt. She scrubbed off the hospital smell and washed her hair with iris-scented shampoo. After wrapping herself in a thick terry robe, she wiped the steam off the mirror. Anger filled her eyes as she looked at the tape covering her stitches. She thought of what Marlene had told her the previous night and remembered the strange call she'd received just before the attack. Maybe the mugger did mistake her for Marlene.

A little makeup performed wonders. Slipping into the softness of the violet cashmere sweater, she carefully pulled the sleeves down over the bruises on her arms.

When she finished dressing, she was virtually starving and was picturing hot waffles with raspberry topping, maybe with some crisp bacon on the side. Surely Marlene was up by now.

Amanda stepped out into the hall. Absolute silence. No sounds came from the kitchen below or the living room. There was just the ticking of the grandfather clock in the downstairs entryway.

She's still in bed. Damn! Amanda stood in front of the master bedroom and knocked loudly. "Marlene! It's two o'clock in the afternoon. Aren't you up yet?" When there was no response, she opened the door and was slapped in the face by a cold wind. It rushed through the open window, bringing with it a swirl of snow and rain. She crossed the room, slammed the window shut, and turned around. Marlene was nowhere in sight. Anxiety began to form like acid in the pit of Amanda's stomach as she surveyed the room. The sheets were in tangled disarray, trailing onto the floor on the right side of the bed. Even in the gloom, she could see spatters of crimson on the tufted headboard. Pillows, with stuffing sticking out through jagged tears, were tossed about. An overturned bottle of vodka had stained the nightstand. On the floor lay a picture of Wolf Eichler, his handsome face smiling through shards of glass. Next to the photograph, Marlene's pajamas formed a sodden pink and red heap. Her slippers were splattered with blood.

Amanda shut her eyes tight and stifled a scream. Standing motionless, she listened, straining to catch any sound.

All she heard was the storm outside and the beating of her own heart.

There was something else, ever so faint. A drip, drip, drip coming from the bathroom. The door was ajar, and a wedge of yellow light spilled onto the carpet. She paused, reluctant to know what might lie a few feet away, then screwed up enough courage to push the bathroom door all the way open. She stood for a moment, shaking uncontrollably. Repressing tears, she took another cautious step. Her nostrils were assaulted by the flowery fragrance of soap mingled with a coppery stench.

The soft dripping now seemed to roar in her ears. Amanda held her breath and crept farther into the pink marble room. Her foot struck a silver hairbrush. Skittering across the floor, it crashed into the matching mirror. She stood stock-still.

"Marlene." Amanda's voice sounded hollow and strange. She now had a full view of the large bathtub. It sat on top of a marble platform, completely encircled by pink silk. "Marlene," she said again.

Filled with dread, she pulled back the curtain.

Marlene's large, lovely eyes stared up at Amanda with the unblinking gaze of death. Under the showerhead, streaks of blood covered the marble tiles as if Marlene had tried to climb the wall to escape her fate. She had been stabbed over and over again, and her throat had been cut. Even her lips were covered with blood. Crimson water half filled the bathtub.

Amanda doubled over and started to retch, but there was nothing in her stomach. Only a bitter fluid came up the back of her throat and onto her tongue. She erupted into dry heaves that shook her entire body until finally subsiding into shivers. Someone had violently cut Marlene to ribbons while Amanda slept peacefully, knocked out by drugs and vodka. How long did he stay? How did he get in? Was he still here hiding, ready to stab her, too?

CHAPTER 5

Taking short, shallow breaths, Amanda slipped out of the bathroom, averting her eyes as she passed the bloody bed and pajamas. She paused at the doorway leading into the hall, listening. All was quiet, except for the ticking of the grandfather clock below. After several minutes, she edged toward the top of the stairs. She half ran half fell down the steps to the front door. Fighting with the locks, she finally escaped into the courtyard. Her eyes were flooded with tears and rain as she stumbled to a neighboring duplex and rang and rang the bell.

After what seemed forever, Greta Kapps came to the door still groggy from her afternoon nap. The elderly widow peered out through the slight opening allowed by the chain lock. "Who is it?

"Help me. Marlene Eichler has been murdered!"

"Murdered? Oh, my God. I will telephone the police

at once." Frau Kapps scurried away. After a few minutes, she came back. "They have asked to speak to you. Oh, forgive me, please come in."

Wet and shaky, Amanda picked up the receiver. An officious voice asked a barrage of questions and told her to stay there until the kommissar of police could speak with her. She put down the phone and leaned back against the wall.

"You poor child. Come into the kitchen," Frau Kapps said. "Let me fix you some hot tea."

❧❧❧

Kommissar Fredrich Grutzmacher's Mercedes pulled up in front of number 85. Two uniformed officers, a pair of German shepherds at their heels, stood guard at the door.

"The body's upstairs, Herr Kommissar."

A small crowd of police and forensic officers were already at work, directed by Unter Kommissar Ernst Rudolf. They were going over the victim's bedroom, centimeter by centimeter. Some vacuumed for hair and particles, others dusted for prints. Precise measurements were being taken of the distances between items in the room. All evidence was bagged and tagged, then carefully placed into containers.

Slight of build with neat gray hair, Grutzmacher had a reputation for thoroughness and tenacity. He was well aware that his quiet and exacting methods irritated the new officer from East Germany. Rudolf indicated the location of the body, and the two men walked into the bathroom as the medical officer was packing up.

"What do we have here, Lipke?" Grutzmacher asked, reaching inside his raincoat and pulling out a package of Roth-Händle cigarettes. He carefully removed the cellophane as he listened to Lipke's droning voice.

"Female, between thirty-five and forty, stabbed sixteen times in the arms, legs, and abdomen before her throat was cut." Lipke's black eyes were completely round. His flat bald head and rotund physique reminded Grutzmacher of a frog.

The kommissar put a cigarette into his mouth without lighting it and looked down at the body. His expression concealed that what he saw sickened him. *She was beautiful still*, he thought. *What could she have possibly done to spark such brutality and rage?* He examined the bloody smears behind the tub. "Was she sexually assaulted?"

"I can't be certain until the tests are done." Lipke closed his bag. "Obviously, the murder weapon was some kind of serrated knife. As you can see, it ripped into the flesh rather than making a smooth even cut. The victim is small; I'd estimate less than forty-nine kilograms. It wouldn't take much to overpower her."

"What about time of death?" Grutzmacher asked.

"The cold temperature of the room and the water in

the tub make it difficult to be precise. Between ten last night and maybe one or two o'clock in the morning. I have to go. The sooner I get back to my lab, the sooner the tests will be done."

Grutzmacher waved his hand in Lipke's direction, more a dismissal than goodbye. He studied the victim for another moment then reached down and gently closed her eyes. *What a waste.* He finally lit his cigarette and walked down the stairs followed by Rudolf. He took a deep drag. "Who was she?"

Rudolf snapped open his notebook. "Marlene Eichler, ex-wife of Wolf Eichler. Anyone who reads *Der Stern* magazine would know that was his photograph we found on the floor. He lives in Düsseldorf. Frau Eichler co-owned an art gallery here in Cologne. Her business partner, an American named Amanda Lee, reported finding the body at two-fifteen p.m. She is awaiting interrogation at a neighbor's condo, number eighty-seven. This is her passport. I found it in her handbag on the hall table. Shall we go?"

"I think it's best if I speak to her alone."

"As you wish, Kommissar." Rudolf cursed under his breath as he stalked outside.

Grutzmacher scanned the living room. Forensics had already been there, leaving traces of powder behind. Two rings from glasses remained on the table. He looked up at Marlene Eichler's portrait. Her eyes smiled down on him, and he wondered what it would be like to be loved by such a woman. Mostly he felt awkward with the fair sex, so he directed all of his energies into his work. It was only during the solitude of evening that he missed the warmth of companionship.

He finished his cigarette and opened the French doors. Locked from the inside, they showed no sign of forced entry. He stepped outside into the bone-chilling rain. No footprints on the grounds or on the patio. Whoever killed Frau Eichler came in through the front door, probably admitted by the victim or her guest. It was time to have a talk with the American woman.

⌒⌒⌒

Amanda had stopped crying and sat motionless in a straight-backed chair. The cheery little kitchen seemed surreal in the context of what was happening. Her gaze fixed on a ceramic pig cookie jar. It stared back with painted eyes.

"You have not touched your tea," Frau Kapps said. "Try to take a few sips. It will make you feel better." The old woman set out another cup. "The kommissar has arrived," she said and left the room.

Without removing his raincoat, he seated himself across the table from Amanda. "Frau Lee? I am Kommissar Fredrich Grutzmacher." He inclined his head slightly as he introduced himself, and then he placed a small tape recorder between them. She watched a drop of rain crawl, snail-like, down the front of his coat, leaving a damp trail. "Would you state your full name and address, please?"

Amanda did as he asked.

"I have just come from the crime scene. Terrible business. A knife is the most personal way to kill. Someone must have hated Frau Eichler a great deal. I understand you were business partners."

"Yes. She invited me to stay with her a few days until I could recuperate."

"Recuperate from what?"

Amanda described how she had been mugged, hospitalized, and released into Marlene's care. She stopped to moisten her throat with a sip of tepid tea.

"Who would want to kill her?" Grutzmacher said.

"I don't know. Last night, she told me she'd been receiving strange phone calls. Sometimes the caller would just hang up. Sometimes they would speak to her in a mechanical voice."

"And say what exactly?"

"She didn't tell me, but she was frightened." *Very frightened.* Amanda remembered Marlene's hopeless expression as she'd gone up to bed.

"Did she know who might be making these calls?"

"No."

"And the police were not contacted?"

"Our first big opening is next week. She was afraid it would cause unwanted publicity."

"Did you hear anyone come to the house last night?"

"No. I'm afraid I drank too much on an empty stomach. That, combined with medication, knocked me out cold. I didn't even make it up to the guest room. I slept on the sofa."

"You heard no noise coming from upstairs?"

"No, I didn't." If only she hadn't downed so much vodka, Marlene might still be alive. "The last thing I remember was the clock in the hall striking ten. And—oh yes, the phone rang."

"Frau Eichler answered?"

"I assume she did."

"Was the door locked this afternoon, after you discovered the body?"

"Yes."

"Double bolted?"

"I can't remember."

"How could someone get through the main gate?"

"They'd have to be buzzed in," Amanda said. "There's a buzzer and intercom in the hall, upstairs and down."

"We found no evidence of forced entry. Do you know who might have keys to her condo?"

"No." Her stomach felt queasy. One hand now covered her eyes, trying to make her head ache less. Even so, she realized that someone else had entered the room.

"My dear Kommissar, Frau Lee is obviously not feeling well. Don't you think she has answered enough questions for now?"

That voice could only belong to Dieter Becker. Amanda looked up. He stood just inside the doorway. At fifty-five, Dieter exuded an air of power and elegance, although his form and features were quite ordinary. Silver touched the bright red of his hair, softening the ruddy complexion.

"Dieter!" Amanda had never been so glad to see anyone in her life.

He strode across the room and put a protective arm around her shoulders.

"What are you doing here, Herr Becker?" Grutzmacher asked.

"You know that, as a member of the press, albeit an arts editor, I have access to police calls and other sources," Dieter said. "Marlene Eichler and I were good friends." He looked compassionately at Amanda. "Surely you can't believe Frau Lee had anything to do with what's happened?"

"Sir, your friend has been murdered in a most horrific way," Grutzmacher said. "We have to question everyone acquainted with Frau Eichler as a matter of course. By the way, Herr Becker, where were you last night?"

"I attended a formal dinner at the Berlin Arts Club. Between nine and ten, I was making a speech to one hundred and fifty collectors. Afterward, I drove back to Cologne, where I spent most of the night getting out my column."

Grutzmacher looked at Amanda. "You may go for

now, but I must ask you not to plan any trips." He held up Amanda's passport. "We will hold onto this for the time being."

❦

Amanda grasped Dieter's arm as they shared his umbrella and hurried across the courtyard. "I must pick up my things," Amanda said as they passed number eighty-five.

"The condo is a crime scene Amanda, they won't let you enter."

Two attendants were placing Marlene's body into an ambulance. Amanda hid her face in Dieter's chest. She had never felt so utterly alone. With Marlene's remains gone from view, the curiosity seekers fixed their gaze on Dieter. A ripple of excitement moved through the on-lookers as they recognized him from his television show. Then their attention fell on Amanda. He shielded her with his bulk as they headed toward his Mercedes.

Inside the car, Amanda felt insulated from everything. Dieter turned on the ignition, and the soothing strains of "Liebestraum No. 3" flowed from the speakers. The soft leather of the seat was comforting as she leaned back and closed her eyes.

Dieter reached over and squeezed her hand. "Don't worry, Amanda. I won't let anything happen to you."

It felt good to let someone else take over. Even

though she didn't know what he could do, she felt reassured by his presence. She knew a few people in Cologne, but she hadn't been close to anyone except Marlene. Most all of her time was spent at the gallery, building their fledgling business. There was no one in the States she could call. She'd stopped communicating with friends in New York after she was jilted. *If only my parents were still alive.*

"When did you last eat?" Dieter asked.

She opened her eyes. They were speeding along the Autobahn toward Cologne proper. "Yesterday noon, I think."

"Well, I insist you eat something. Dinner is a few hours off, but I think I can persuade Herr Aurich to fix us a little snack."

"No, Dieter, I couldn't. I just want to go home."

"You've got to eat," he said as he turned off at the next exit onto Aachener Strasse.

Within minutes they pulled up in front of the Kunstler Cafe. Amanda knew Dieter spent a fortune there, wining and dining artists and notables, as well as his many friends. She and Marlene had joined him on occasion. Dieter knocked on the door. They were given an effusive welcome and shown to the table where Dieter usually held forth. The proprietor, Herr Aurich, handed them each a *Speisekarte* listing numerous specialties.

"What would you like, my dear?" Dieter asked.

"Just some tea."

Herr Aurich's jolly face smiled above a spotless white apron.

"She'll have asparagus soup with bread and some chamomile tea," Dieter said. "I'll have a Kölner Pils and a dozen oysters on the half shell."

The tea settled Amanda's stomach, and the soup gave her strength. It was Dieter who had trouble eating, barely touching his food.

"I'm sorry, Dieter. I've been so concerned with my own loss, I didn't stop to think how much you loved Marlene. You were friends for a long time."

His face softened. "Since she was seventeen years old."

"Then you knew her about the time she left the orphanage?"

"I helped her get away from that place. The head mistress used to lock her up at night to keep her from going out. They dispensed discipline with a leather switch."

"How did you two meet?"

Dieter's eyes took on a little of their old sparkle. "She stood waiting for me out in front of the News Building with a copy of the paper folded to my column. She walked right up to me and said, 'Herr Becker, I'm Marlene Kumpf, and I want to learn all about art.' I found out later her given name was Frieda; she renamed herself after her idol, Marlene Dietrich. At first, I brushed her aside. I had no time for a teenager with a head full of nonsense. But she was a charmer even then. She used that incredible way she had, and I ended up taking her to lunch and promising to help."

"You taught her a lot."

"Everything I know, and that, my dear, is considerable. I took her in, and for over a year, we discussed art night and day, visited every museum, went to every opening. I introduced her to most of the artists and collectors with whom I am acquainted. I even taught her how to dress, how to behave."

"You sound like Henry Higgins."

"Yes, it was a bit like that. When I thought she was ready, I got her a job at the Wallraf-Richartz Museum, where she met her first husband. He was an Austrian—related to the Habsburgs, I believe. It was then I realized her primary interest in art was the access it gave her to wealthy men."

"You must have been disappointed," Amanda said.

"Oh, I was at first, but I got over it. Marlene's husbands were the ones who suffered."

Herr Aurich came to take away the dishes. He frowned at the expensive oysters left uneaten on Dieter's plate.

"Another beer for me, and more tea for Frau Lee, please," Dieter said. He turned to Amanda. "Did Marlene tell you anything that could give us a clue as to who might have done this?"

"She'd been getting anonymous phone calls. I'm not sure for how long."

"Anything else?"

She thought for a moment. "Yes! She said she'd received a package at the gallery. Some kind of sick joke."

"Did she describe the contents of this package?"

"No."

"Did you mention it to the police?"

"I didn't think of it until now."

Dieter called for the check. "Let's go."

Amanda put on her coat. The gallery was only a short distance away. As they drove down the Pfeilstrasse, it was all but deserted. The pounding rain had swept the streets of all Sunday window shoppers. Dieter pulled into the parking lot, and Amanda's muscles tightened as she looked at the spot where she'd been attacked. Her old VW was still where she'd left it.

୧୬୧୬

Inside, the atmosphere would have been eerie even without the Kruger paintings. Shadows of the raindrops on the windows slid down the walls and canvases as if the entire gallery wept.

Dieter flipped on the light switch and stopped for a moment to take in the magnitude of the Kruger show. "Very impressive." He followed Amanda into the office. "Do you have any idea what we are looking for? Is the package large, small, flat, square?"

"I don't know."

They rummaged through file drawers and both desks but came away empty-handed. They checked the storage room, the vault, the restroom, and the assistant's desk. After a thorough search, they had found nothing out of the ordinary.

"Well, we've looked everywhere," Amanda said. "Marlene's package isn't here. We might as well leave."

They put on their coats and headed for the door. As Dieter switched off the lights, a single spotlight turned on in the catwalk gallery. Amanda was afraid to move.

"There's no one there. That light must be on a timer," Dieter said.

They walked up the staircase leading to the catwalk. With each step, Amanda's anxiety grew. They passed half a dozen small paintings by Kruger. Finally, they came to the spotlighted work. It was as if the mugger's hand had again covered Amanda's nose and mouth. A silent scream clawed the inside of her throat. The canvas was about seventy-five by ninety centimeters and framed in black-lacquered wood. The brush strokes were bold but well defined. The vibrant colors had a painfully vivid quality, a style reminiscent of the American painter Edward Hopper.

Depicted in grim detail was Marlene, just as Amanda had found her: long blonde hair draped across the rim of the bathtub, the stab wounds, the crimson water, the whole horrific scene.

CHAPTER 6

Amanda sank onto the office sofa. A growing sorrow left her feeling lost and empty. "Why did he copy Hopper's style?"

"Probably to avoid his personal style being recognized."

"Oh, God. If Marlene had only confided in me sooner, perhaps…"

Dieter poured them each a brandy. "What could you do? You were in the hospital. She obviously didn't want to upset you."

"And you were out of town."

"Regrettably, yes. When did this package arrive?"

"Yesterday afternoon, a little before she picked me up. It was obvious then that something was terribly wrong. I don't know when the anonymous calls started, but she received one around six p.m. on Thursday. We had just returned from my makeover and shopping. Later that evening, I was mugged. Marlene thought that someone had mistaken me for her."

"I must say, you now look enough like her that, in dim light, I could be fooled," Dieter said. "Well, if anyone can find out who's behind all this, it will be Fredrich Grutzmacher. Maybe I can help him track down the person who created that painting. After all, I am Germany's foremost art critic." Dieter smiled at Amanda, patting her hand. "I'll give Fredrich a call, report the painting, and volunteer my services."

Amanda nodded. "I'll help in any way I can."

"Right now you look exhausted. I think you should go home. I'll wait here for the police."

"Perhaps I should stay and talk to them too," Amanda said.

"That's not necessary. I can handle everything and lock up when we're finished."

A bolt of lightning flashed, preceding a loud crash of thunder that caused the windows to chatter like frightened monkeys. Trees thrashed in the escalating wind. Amanda felt shaky and sick. She didn't feel up to another encounter with the police. She pulled an extra set of keys from her desk drawer and gave them to Dieter.

"The security code is thirty, thirty-eight, my age and Marlene's."

"I'll call you a taxi. I don't think you should be driving," Dieter said.

"I prefer to take my own car."

ℒℕℒℕ

Arriving home, she hurried through her private entrance on the ground floor and double-locked the door. After making a cup of tea, she dropped down on the sofa bed she'd gotten from Ikea. Aside from a table, chair, and chest of drawers, that was pretty much it for furniture. She hadn't expected to buy a gallery and stay in Germany when she'd moved in, so she had bought cheap, make-do items. The same was true of her car.

Her apartment was the first one she found at a reasonable rent after she and Karl split up. Unpacked boxes, still stacked in one corner of the room, hid behind a three-panel screen. Several contemporary works of art sat on the bare floor, still waiting to be hung.

Shuffling sounds at the door caused Amanda to jump and almost drop the teacup. A piece of folded paper was pushed through the mail slot and landed on the floor. She went over and picked it up.

Dear Frau Lee. Your lease is up, and I cannot extend it. My son requires the use of this apartment.

It was from Frau Pouls, the landlady. Stamped in red were the words *Second Notice*. Rental apartments were difficult to find. Amanda had been so busy at the gallery, she'd put off looking for one and then forgotten about it. She let the unwelcome reminder slide from her hands back to the floor. Exhaustion overtook body and mind, temporarily blocking out the recent past. She curled up on the sofa bed and fell asleep.

℘℘

"Frau Eichler was not raped, so we have no semen sample," Lipke said. "There was nothing under her fingernails—no skin or hair. All the blood samples taken from the crime scene belonged to the victim. Whoever did this took care not to leave us any mementos. The victim was very intoxicated at the time of death. Her stomach was empty, and her blood alcohol level was point-two-one." He laid his autopsy report on the edge of the kommissar's desk. "I've been working for thirty-six hours straight, and I'm going home. I've made every conceivable test. There's nothing more we can learn. I'm releasing the body for burial."

Grutzmacher watched the medical examiner's broad back disappear through the wavy glass of his office door. Perhaps he should have another talk with Frau Lee.

℘℘

It was past six p.m. and already dark. A persistent drizzle coated the gallery windows with a glistening residue. Amanda's mood was as gloomy as the weather. She was preparing to close when a car pulled up in front, the tires making a whooshing sound in the rain. The sole occupant got out, enveloped in a droopy raincoat—it was Grutzmacher.

She opened the door, and he entered, apologizing for not calling ahead.

"I took a chance that you might still be here," he said. "I have some questions I need answered to help with our investigation."

Amanda's weariness gave way to a chilling disquiet as she showed him into the office. "Here, let me take your coat. Would you like some coffee? It will only take a minute."

"No thank you." He pulled out his little tape recorder and placed it on the desk between them. His presence enhanced the continuing nightmare of Marlene's death. Amanda struggled to present a calm demeanor.

"Frau Lee, what kind of relationship did you have with your late business partner?"

"We were on good terms."

"Did you ever argue over issues related to the gallery, finances perhaps?"

"No, we were in agreement on practically everything. We each had our separate roles to play."

Grutmacher scrutinized her face through narrowed eyes. "I see." He took a pack of cigarettes out of his pocket. "Do you mind?"

"I'd rather you didn't."

"How about her dealings with Wolf Eichler?"

"They were cordial. Marlene was sorry they'd divorced."

"According to the neighbors, they lived in the murder condo for less than a year. Did he still visit her there on occasion?"

"I don't know."

"Was she seeing a particular man at the time of her death?"

"She didn't usually discuss these things with me, except for—"

"Except for what?"

"The night she died she mentioned two men. She had just broken off an affair with Hans Demuth."

"Isn't he the one who married the Vogt Steel heiress? It was in all the papers at the time."

"Yes. Marlene said he was furious and later threatened her, but she thought he was too spineless to be taken seriously."

"Continue."

"She saw him for dinner the Thursday before her death, that's all I know."

Grutzmacher toyed with an unlit cigarette. "You mentioned there were two men."

"The second one was more mysterious—someone from Berlin whom she'd met recently. She didn't tell me his name, only that he became controlling and abusive. She said he was starting to creep her out."

"Did she say where she met this man?"

"No."

"Frau Lee, I must ask for our records. Did you kill your business partner? You were on the scene, you discovered the body, and, according to her attorney, you inherit Frau Eichler's half of this lucrative business. People have committed murder for far less."

Tears began to flow through cracks in her tenuous calm. "No, no, of course, I didn't."

As Grutzmacher left the gallery, he did not believe Frau Lee could commit such an act, but then he had to keep an open mind and go where the evidence led him. He would get to Demuth at some point. As for the mystery man, they had nothing to go on. Wolf Eichler seemed the more likely suspect. Rudolf's sources in Düsseldorf had informed them that the divorce was messy and expensive. They needed to check out Herr Eichler, down to what he ate for breakfast.

ℰℐℰℐ

The next morning, sitting at his desk, Grutzmacher examined a small lapis and gold tuxedo stud found embedded between the bedroom wall and the carpet of the murder condo. It was a simple oval, expensive but not showy. Armed with photos of Eichler and the stud, Rudolf and his men were trying to locate the jeweler or auction house that had sold it.

And, of course, there was the death painting. If

Becker located the artist, that would be all they'd need. However, Grutzmacher knew he couldn't count on that.

The hot ash of his cigarette burned his finger. "Damn." He picked up the phone and dialed Rudolf's extension. "Have you located the ex-husband? I want him questioned as soon as possible."

❦❦

The sun was bright, the air crisp and invigorating as Wolf Eichler got out of a taxi and hurried toward the recently completed Eichler Building. It had received as much critical acclaim as the superbly elegant Thyssenhaus. He loved the clean look of steel and glass, the straight lines reaching for the sky. To him, it spoke of the new Germany: modern, wealthy, the economic power that would propel Europe into the most exciting era anyone had ever known.

He ran up the granite stairs leading to the impressive entrance, flanked on either side by free-form bronze sculptures commissioned from Franz Stüler. A private elevator hummed its way to the top floor and opened onto custom gray carpeting and glass doors on which Eichler Associates, Architects was written in silver letters.

At forty-one, Wolf Eichler looked ten years younger, even though a few strands of gray now laced his ash-blond hair. He was trim, with a six-foot frame that accentuated his straight carriage and showed off his custom-tailored suits. Intense blue eyes lit up the strong features of his face.

"Good morning, Monika."

The curvy young receptionist gave him an openly inviting smile. Frau Witt, his secretary, frowned her disapproval and followed him into his office carrying a silver tray.

"Mmmm, that coffee smells wonderful, and you look particularly fetching today," he said.

Frau Witt ignored the compliment and poured the coffee into a Meissen cup. She had carefully arranged his mail, newspapers, and a handful of messages.

"What's this? I called in each day from Amsterdam. Why didn't you tell me about these?"

She smoothed her sensible brown suit over an ample figure. "I gave you the important messages, Herr Eichler. I try not to bother you with things that can wait until your return."

Wolf knew Frau Witt heartily disliked Marlene and felt it her duty to protect him from "unnecessary distractions." He leafed through the six messages. She'd probably phoned his home as well. He had decided to spend a long weekend in Holland, coming straight to the office from the airport.

"That's all for now, Frau Witt. I need an hour to collect my thoughts, then I want a meeting with the staff." He held up his briefcase in victory, his face breaking into a wide grin. "Eichler Associates will be designing the new Van Dam Arts Museum in Amsterdam."

"Congratulations, sir." Witt gave him a thin-lipped smile then left him to his newspapers and mail.

Wolf sat down at his desk. He reached for the telephone, paused, and picked up the coffee instead. He didn't want to make the call. For a little while, he allowed himself to relive the intense and bittersweet happiness he'd shared with Marlene. She had been the most delectable creature he'd ever met, but under the sophistication was a vulnerable child with many needs. They'd met in late June at *documenta* 6. He'd decided on the spur of the moment to go to Kassel for the art show.

Marlene had come up behind him as he studied a work by American artist Robert Langley. "If you are here as a collector, I would recommend this artist," she said. "His paintings will be worth a fortune one day."

When he turned in the direction of the throaty voice, there was spontaneous combustion. They enjoyed the rest of the show together.

After a candlelight dinner at the Schloss Restaurant, they went to his suite in a converted Rapunzel-type tower that sat high on a hill overlooking the Rhine. Their lovemaking was gentle at first, then Marlene became almost violent, digging her nails into his flesh. He was pleased that he inspired such passion. For a long time afterward, she lay next to him, her hair across his chest. She made a sleepy request for champagne and fresh strawberries, which he ordered from room service. He slipped on his robe to answer the door, and when he returned, she was gone.

He found her standing on the small, circular balcony. She was still nude, moonlight dancing over her body. They sipped wine and kissed in silence as the summer wind stirred the fragrant darkness around them. He had never known anyone like her. He thought that she was a priceless original, a gift from the gods.

He soon discovered, however, that one man would never be enough for her. She needed constant assurance that she was desirable, and it had to come from the lips of new conquests. The affairs started only two months after the wedding. The initial sense of betrayal gave way to the sad realization that sex was both a game and a sickness with her. She couldn't help herself. He repeatedly asked her to see a psychiatrist, but she went into hysterics each time it was mentioned.

He neglected his business to spend more time with her, took her on trips, bought her whatever she wanted, but nothing worked. After each indiscretion, she'd cry as if her heart would break and beg his forgiveness. It was a destructive nightmare that couldn't continue. When she refused to file for divorce, he initiated the action himself. Their marriage lasted less than a year. Since then, she had continued to hover in the background, calling him or showing up unexpectedly at inopportune times. She just wouldn't leave him alone.

He picked up the phone and dialed the Lee Eichler

Gallery in Cologne. It rang a long time. He was about to hang up when he heard the voice of Marlene's partner.

"Frau Lee, Wolf Eichler, here. I am returning Marlene's call. May I speak to her please?"

"Then you don't know."

"Know what?"

"I'm sorry to have to tell you this, but Marlene is dead."

"Oh, my God! How did it happen? Was there an accident?"

"She…she was murdered. I found the body yesterday afternoon. I think it's better if we meet in person rather than talk on the phone."

"Yes, of course. I'll leave for Cologne at once. I should be there in forty-five minutes."

A surge of feelings—shock, guilt, sorrow for the loss of a dream that could not survive—overtook him. As he sat quietly with eyes closed, he realized he felt something else—a deep sense of relief.

∽∾∽

A Swedish masseuse pummeled Helga Demuth's large hips as she lay face down on a padded table. Handel played in the background. Soft female voices passing in the corridor flowed in and out of the music.

Strong hands moved up her back, working scented oil between the shoulder blades. "Madam is very tense this morning. You must relax, relax." The woman helped Helga roll over on her back and lowered the lights. "I'll be back shortly to start your facial."

It was all over now. Marlene Eichler was dead, and Hans was hers once more. Did he not think that she'd find out about his little affair? Her friends had been only too happy to tell her each time they'd seen Hans with that hussy.

Helga felt her muscles tense and her eyes burn with anger. It was high time Hans knew that she knew.

✥✥✥

Amanda waited in the gallery for Wolf Eichler to arrive. After placing the *Closed* sign on the door, she called Rolf to tell him what had happened, but he already knew about Marlene from the local media.

A few minutes later Dieter called. "I had a very good meeting with Fredrich Grutzmacher, and he has accepted our offer to help him find the artist. Forensics went over every centimeter of the death painting. From what I could tell, they found no fingerprints. I was allowed to keep the work a few hours to study it."

"Where is it now?"

"I put it in your storeroom for safekeeping."

"*What*? Just having that thing nearby makes my skin crawl."

"It's only paint and canvas, my dear. It can't hurt

you. I've contacted Fredrich's office. Someone will be there soon to take it off your hands."

"It can't be soon enough."

"By the way, they've finished with the autopsy and are ready to release Marlene's body."

"I'll have to make plans for the funeral," Amanda said.

"Perhaps it'll be easier for me to do that. In fact, I've already made a phone call to the Hofer Funeral Home, and they will pick up our little Marlene this afternoon. Could you select something for her to wear?"

"Yes, of course."

"I thought the small chapel at the dom would be nice for the service. It's available Friday morning at ten. If that's agreeable, I'll confirm the arrangements."

"So soon?" Amanda said.

"Marlene would have wanted it that way," Dieter said.

"All right then, go ahead, and thanks again for everything. I have to go now, Dieter."

Wolf Eichler's Mercedes was pulling up in front of the gallery. Amanda made coffee and Wolf listened quietly as she told him the circumstances surrounding Marlene's death.

"My poor, fragile Marlene. Oh, God." He paused a moment to control his feelings. "And what about you?" he said. "You must have been terrified. Do the police have any idea who might have done this?"

"Not as far as I know." Amanda did not want to add to his grief by mentioning the death painting. She gave him the time and place of the funeral.

"I'll be there," he said. "Meanwhile, you take good care. Until the police get to the bottom of this, you may also be in danger."

Amanda walked Wolf to the door.

He lingered for a moment, as if he wanted to share something. Instead, he handed her his card. "If I can be of help."

"Thank you." She watched for a moment as he drove away.

☙☙☙

The canvas was in the storeroom just as Dieter said, loosely wrapped in brown paper. It was difficult to look at it again, but she must try to be detached. Taking a deep breath, she removed the wrapping.

Whoever painted this had emulated Edward Hopper perfectly—the melancholy, the spareness, and the tension of that style.

Warm tones of flesh and blood stood out from the cold blue of sinister shadows stretching across the floor, claiming first a corner, then a wall. The composition's eroticism was evident in the play of light across the breasts, abdomen, and slightly splayed legs.

Why had this been painted? Was the killer the artist, or had he commissioned the work?

Either way, find the artist, and you find the killer.

ℰↁℰↁ

That night, Amanda awoke from a fitful sleep. At first, she wasn't sure if she'd heard something or only dreamed it. Lying alone in the dark, fear spread through her like an electrical shock. She listened intently. There was nothing but the awful silence that came in the wee hours of the morning. She was slowly drifting back to sleep when she heard them. *Footsteps!* Leaves crunched softly as someone moved to the corner of the building and back. A small circle of yellow light crawled over the window. There was a muffled creaking sound. Someone was trying to get in.

CHAPTER 7

Kommissar Grutzmacher found it soothing to look down at the Rhine. From his office window, it looked like a silver ribbon winding through the city, on its way to Koblenz and beyond. He took a sip of lukewarm coffee and forced his gaze from the beauty of the river to the grim photos neatly displayed on his corkboard. They still hadn't located the murder weapon, although his men had searched the condo, the garden, the garbage cans, and every centimeter of ground surrounding the entire complex.

Grutzmacher's thoughts were interrupted as Rudolf knocked twice and entered the office without waiting for a reply. "I need a couple more men to help track down the source of that lapis and gold stud. We're trying to cover a lot of territory here, and I can't—"

"You've got them," Grutzmacher said as he eyed an

unlit Roth-Händle. He had limited himself to six cigarettes a day, and it would be an hour before he could light
up again. "Did you question Herr Eichler?"

"Yes. He said he was in Amsterdam at the time of
the murder. Of course, he could've easily driven to Cologne that night, killed his ex-wife, and returned to his
hotel. It's only about two hundred kilometers each way.
He says he ate alone at the Excelsior Restaurant and was
there until around ten p.m. He then returned to the Hotel
de L'Europe, where he watched television and went to
bed at midnight.

"I'm going to Amsterdam myself to check on it. To
my mind, he should be a prime suspect. His ex-wife
cheated on him constantly. Her indiscreet behavior
caused him a great deal of professional and personal humiliation. He also had to cough up a very large alimony
payment every month, in addition to a generous settlement and their condo.

"Since he lived there for a year, he might still have a
set of keys, which would account for no forced entry."
Rudolf walked over to the board displaying the photos
and stood at ease with his hands behind his back. "The
American woman is also on my short list," he said. "She
was on the premises and had plenty of opportunities. And
she had an excellent motive—money."

⌘⌘⌘

"My God, Amanda, you look awful," Dieter said, as he breezed into the gallery.

"I didn't sleep well last night," Amanda said. "Someone was creeping around my window with a flashlight."

"Did you call the police?"

"Yes. They came over but didn't find anyone. The intruder must have run away when he heard them approaching. The officer in charge insisted it was all a bad dream."

"Maybe it was. You're under a lot of stress. The mind plays tricks."

"I was not dreaming."

"No, of course not." He cleared his throat. "I just popped in to see how you are and to tell you everything is all set for Friday morning. I had to pull a few strings to have her service at the dom, and it took a major contribution for them to agree to what I consider a proper sendoff. She wasn't religious, you know. I also put a notice in my column along with a brief tribute."

At the thought of Marlene, a renewed sadness tugged at Amanda's soul. A best friend lost, her life summed up in a brief tribute. The next few weeks were going to be among the most difficult Amanda had ever faced.

"I must say you did a beautiful job of mounting the Kruger show," he said, looking around the gallery. "It will be a huge success."

"Don't you think that, out of respect for Marlene, we

should cancel it or at least postpone it for a while?"

"Absolutely not! After all the publicity I've given this—on my television show, in my column—not to mention the money and effort you and Marlene put in. The biggest collectors are coming. Cancellation is impossible at this point."

"I'm not sure it's right."

"You know as well as I do that Marlene would have wanted us to go forward with the show. I think it is a fitting tribute to her."

"A show about death?"

"Death is part of life." He softened his voice. "I know this has been difficult for you, but you can't afford to disappoint the caliber of people who've accepted. They would never forgive you or me. This show will bring in a lot of money, and you're going to need it." He gave her arm a reassuring pat. "I'll be there to help you, from beginning to end."

Later that day, Amanda received a call from Marlene's lawyer. "Good afternoon Frau Lee, Herr Betz here. Has Frau Eichler's funeral been scheduled?"

"We've just finalized the arrangements," Amanda said and gave him the details.

"Well," he said, "she requested that her will be read immediately following her funeral. Is one o'clock at my office convenient?"

"Yes."

After Amanda hung up, she walked over to Marlene's desk and went through its meager contents once more. The top drawer contained a Chanel lipstick, nail enamel, paper clips, and a few pencils. There was nothing much in the other drawers either. She wasn't sure what she was looking for. Then she remembered Marlene's diary. Where was it? She barely used the computer, so her diary contained every appointment, every detail of her busy life. Perhaps the police took it. According to Dieter, they had searched the office and the gallery thoroughly the night the death painting was found. Amanda had a strong feeling the killer's name was written on one of its pages.

∽∾∽

Amanda held onto Dieter's arm as they walked through the massive church. A bishop nodded a silent greeting then, ghostlike, disappeared into a darkened recess. The Gothic gloom of the Kölner Dom was offset by its mysterious beauty. The nave, side aisles, transept, and choir exhibited ecclesiastical treasures dating back to the Middle Ages. Light from ancient stained glass windows splashed jewel-like colors onto the sanctuary. Behind the high altar, the reliquary of the Three Holy Kings, completed in 1220, was resplendent with gold and precious stones. In order to screw up her courage to face the funeral, Amanda stopped and took several deep breaths.

"Are you all right?" Dieter asked.

"I think so."

As they entered the chapel, they heard the Adagio from Mozart's "Clarinet Concerto." It came from behind golden damask draperies, where the musicians were secreted. Placed in front of the fifteenth-century altarpiece, the rosewood casket was surrounded on three sides by candles and all-white flowers: orchids, roses, giant tulips, and camellias. Their combined fragrances permeated the air.

Marlene's face was serene, as if she were having a pleasant dream. The paleness of her silky hair fell soft and lose around her face. The burgundy empire dress with high neckline and long tight sleeves hid the ugliness of murder. A square-cut ruby ring gleamed from her right hand, which rested over her heart.

Amanda leaned over and kissed Marlene's forehead for the last time. "Farewell, dear friend," she whispered. She stifled a sob and took a seat in the first row.

Dieter also kissed Marlene and sat next to Amanda. Wolf arrived and stood for a few moments, looking down at his ex-wife. He caressed her cheek and chose a place across the aisle.

Neighbors, collectors, and gallery owners paid their respects—far more men than women. Sophia Danielle was there as was Rolf, his eyes rimmed with red. As the service was about to begin, two men slipped into seats in the last row. Amanda recognized one as Grutzmacher. The other one she didn't know, but from his demeanor, she assumed that he too was with the police. The priest said prayers and a mass of Christian burial. This was followed by Dieter's touching eulogy about the "little Marlene" he'd known.

Then Amanda went to the podium. Her mouth felt dry, and it was hard to project her voice. "I'd like to read one of Marlene's favorite poems from a book her mother gave her many years ago." She opened the thin volume to a place marked by a faded ribbon and read.

> "'As fragile as a trembling reed
> Bending toward the stream,
> Gentle as a summer breeze,
> Pale as a moonbeam.
> Soft and fragrant as a flower,
> Lovely as a song,
> She graced this earth but for an hour,
> Then like the mist was gone.'"

A few tears escaped from beneath Amanda's lashes as she returned to her seat.

"Eternal rest, grant to her, O Lord." The priest's voice reverberated throughout the chapel. "Let perpetual light shine upon her, and may she rest in peace."

❧❧❧

Herr Adam Betz, attorney-at-law, cleared his throat

for attention and raised his bushy eyebrows, which formed impressive arches over round, metal-framed glasses. "Herr Becker is unable to be here," he said. "Important business at the newspaper." He began the reading of the will. "'To my beloved Wolf, I leave the condo at Wagner Court, where we shared the happiest moments of my life. I also leave him the furnishings and the large portrait of myself, which hangs over the mantle there. Perhaps he will look at it and think of his Marlene once in a while.'"

Amanda glanced at Wolf. He wore a weary expression. She got the feeling he would rather not have inherited these constant reminders of his ex-wife. Poor Marlene had loved him so much she tried to hang on even after death.

To Amanda, she left her half of the business. The two partners had agreed to make each other beneficiaries for all business interests, and this was not a surprise. Neither of them had a family. The next part, however, was completely unexpected. "'I also bequeath to my dearest friend, Amanda Lee, all of my personal property, jewels, furs, clothes, and my car.

"'To my old friend Dieter, I leave the Joseph Bueys painting he gave me many years ago.'" Herr Betz cleared his throat once more. "I'm afraid her bank account barely contains enough to take care of outstanding bills. Marlene was not a big believer in saving money."

"If additional funds are needed," Wolf said, "I will provide them."

As they left the lawyer's office, Amanda felt adrift in an alien sea. What would the future hold? Perhaps when this was all over, she would sell the gallery and go back to the States. One thing was certain—Marlene's murderer would have to be caught before she could entertain any ideas of going home.

Outside, Wolf asked her to join him for a late lunch. "I think we could both use a glass of wine as well."

He smiled at Amanda with such warmth, that for a moment, she was transported out of her dismal frame of mind.

They decided on the Klimt Cafe near the gallery. The place was unusually quiet, which Amanda welcomed. They sat for a few minutes without saying anything. While she scanned the menu, she could feel him studying her.

"I thought your reading very touching," he said when they had ordered. "Marlene would have been most pleased."

"I hope so. She was very good to me and changed my life in many positive ways. I had no idea how much I'd miss her."

"When would you like the clothing and other items she left you? I can have them sent over. I believe the police have finished with the condo."

"I hope I can leave everything there for now,"

Amanda said. "My lease is up in a week, and I must find somewhere else to live."

"That won't be easy on short notice, especially if you want to rent."

The waiter brought a bottle of chilled Riesling, showed it to Wolf, then poured two glasses.

"I have a suggestion that I know may seem a bit strange, but at least consider it," Wolf continued.

"Yes?"

"Why don't you move into Marlene's condo? I can have the place completely cleaned and refurbished in just five or six days. Being an architect has its advantages."

"I don't know," Amanda said. "Marlene was murdered in that place."

"This is true. But as you just heard Herr Betz read from her will, it was also the place where she was most happy. I'm sure she would have wanted you to stay there."

"I just can't."

"Of course. If it makes you uncomfortable, then perhaps it's not a good idea. I just thought…well, the place is lovely, and it seems a shame for it to sit empty when you need somewhere to live."

"What if the killer comes back?"

"If you decide to move in, I'll order a very elaborate security system. Once it's installed, you would be safer there than anywhere else."

"No, I couldn't. But thank you for the offer."

"I understand," he said, his blue eyes meeting hers. "I just wanted to help."

"I'll call some real estate agents. I'm sure I'll find something," Amanda said.

The next morning, Amanda called several brokers and was told that finding a decent one-bedroom rental or even a studio would require her being put on a waiting list. Of course, "key money" would speed up the process.

She asked them to call her if something suitable came up. After that, she and Rolf were deluged with preparations for Kruger's reception party and show the following Thursday.

CHAPTER 8

That Thursday evening, there was a full moon and not a hint of rain, a perfect night for a gala opening. Amanda wore the beige French angora dress she and Marlene had selected only weeks before. She loved the sparkle of small crystal beads scattered over the soft knit—something she would never have chosen on her own. She'd kept her appointment with Ute Bauer, and her hair looked sleek and sophisticated. In this light, it was almost the same shade as the dress.

The best caterers in Cologne were setting up the bar under the catwalk. Long tables draped in fresh white linen gleamed with Rosenthal crystal. Standing like soldiers in ice chests beneath the tables were bottles of Perrier-Jouët Fleur de Champagne. Canapés were to be passed among the guests by waiters wearing gloves and short white jackets.

Kruger wanted his paintings draped, to be revealed by him for dramatic effect. Scheduled to participate in the unveiling was his Asian mistress. Rolf had been there all afternoon putting sheet-like fabric over the larger works in the main gallery and setting up a movable spotlight on the catwalk that would follow the artist from painting to painting. The wealthiest collectors, prominent people from Cologne, Düsseldorf, and Berlin, had all sent their intentions to attend the invitation-only affair. Most were Dieter's friends. Part of the event would be recorded by a camera crew and appear later on his television show. True to his word, Dieter was the first to arrive.

"You look ravishing," he said, kissing Amanda on both cheeks. Dieter himself was perfectly turned out in a custom-made tuxedo. Black Tahitian pearl studs dotted the front of his pleated white shirt. His eyes danced with excitement as he directed his crew where to set up the cameras. "This will be a night to remember!" He nodded approval as he checked the champagne then inspected the way each painting was draped.

Amanda was too numb to be nervous. She just hoped she could get through the evening. At seven o'clock, she heard the slamming of car doors and the laughter that heralded the arrival of the first guests, the Sebastian Spechts of Düsseldorf. Herr Specht's blond goatee was neatly trimmed, his tuxedo perfectly tailored, and his bearing proud and aristocratic. Frau Specht was his perfect feminine counterpart. Right behind them was the chauffeur-driven Bentley of the Baron von Schlegell, who was known for his philanthropic endeavors as well as for his large private art collection.

Dieter was at the door in a second, greeting them effusively. They eyed Amanda with skeptical expressions. For a moment, it was almost comical and caused her to remember something she'd read. Was it P. G. Wodehouse who wrote: *The Germans are tall and blond, but not as tall and blond as they think they are*?

"Herr and Frau Specht, Baron von Schlegell, may I present Amanda Lee, the owner of this gallery and our charming hostess," Dieter said.

"How do you do?" Frau Specht said.

Herr Spect simply nodded in her direction.

With a glint in his eye, the baron kissed her hand.

"I hope that you enjoy the evening," Amanda said, as Dieter summoned champagne for three and moved them into the room.

The doorbell rang, announcing more arrivals. This time it was Herr Doctor Kohlmann accompanied by a dazzling Frau von Zeddelmann. She swept passed Amanda in a flurry of white fox and headed straight for Dieter. "Dieter, it's been ages!"

This was clearly his night, and he was eating it up.

"Helga and Hans Demuth," said the attractive young man, introducing himself and his wife to Amanda.

"How do you do? I hope you enjoy the exhibition."

So this was Hans Demuth. His wife was a marked

contrast to Hans and considerably older. Jewels adorned every finger. Her dress, though obviously expensive, was not flattering. Hans put his arm around his wife and headed in the direction of the other guests.

It was no longer possible for Amanda to greet everyone. The gallery had never held so many people. With each new arrival, the din of conversation and laughter increased. No one seemed to care about the Kruger paintings concealed beneath their shrouds. *Where is Kruger?* Amanda wondered. She'd heard he liked to make grand entrances, but it was already an hour and a half into the evening.

A few minutes later, Dieter ordered the lights turned down. He introduced Amanda and made a dedication to Marlene. Then the gallery became completely dark except for the large movable spotlight controlled by one of the camera crew. A hush fell over the crowd, and they instinctively cleared a path from the entrance to the middle of the room.

The front door flung open, and an exotic beauty entered, wearing a kimono and, from what Amanda could tell, nothing else. She carried a large shallow drum, which she beat with her hand in a slow, measured rhythm. Dark, waist-length hair fell across her face as she dipped and turned with each beat, her eyes trance-like. About three meters into the room, she started a howling cantata that reminded Amanda of a Kabuki soliloquy.

Then Kruger materialized in the doorway. In spite of

the cold, he was naked to the waist, wearing only his dirty green leather pants and an inverted cross earring. His greasy ponytail was tied with a black leather cord. Carefully placing one long bony foot directly in front of the other, he followed the woman into the room, stopping on every third drumbeat to roll his head spastically and pivot around.

The crowd backed out of the way as the strange pair slowly advanced toward the largest painting. When they reached the wall, the woman beat the drum more loudly and quickly then stopped to complete silence. The spotlight narrowed to include only Kruger's skeletal face and penetrating eyes. "Evil, not good, is the food of all great art!" With that, he ripped the covering off the painting of the wolves and the rabbit. The spotlight pulled back to include the painting's full magnitude. "There are those who are meant to survive and those who are meant to die."

Are these people impressed by this ridiculous performance? Amanda thought.

Kruger moved from painting to painting, dramatically unveiling each one, making what he thought were profound statements such as, "Death, not sex, is the ultimate experience."

Amanda suddenly remembered how he came on to Marlene. Had he given her "the ultimate experience?"

CHAPTER 9

It was hard to tell who was the greater con artist, Kruger or Dieter. Nonetheless, Amanda was relieved that the opening was a financial success. Over the course of the evening, small red dots were affixed next to numerous paintings. Dieter was in his glory as he interviewed several well-known collectors. They posed with Kruger in front of their purchases and went on about the importance his art would gain in the future. By the time the last guests departed, Amanda was exhausted.

She got home around ten-thirty and parked her VW in the usual spot. Getting out of the car, she saw the curtains move in a lighted upstairs window and recognized the silhouette of her landlady. What would she do for entertainment when her favorite tenant was gone? Amanda frequently had the feeling that the nosey woman went into her apartment when she wasn't there. Nothing was ever missing, but things seemed to move from one place to another. She had just gotten inside and taken off her shoes when Frau Pouls knocked on the door.

"I was wondering if you've had any luck finding another apartment."

"I'm afraid I haven't," Amanda said.

"Well, I know you've been preoccupied, what with the death of your partner and all. Have the police made any progress?"

"Not that I know of."

"Is it true you were right there, sleeping in the same condo when it happened?"

"Frau Pouls, I'm very tired—"

"Some people say, but, of course, I'm not one to judge, that Frau Eichler went to after-hours clubs. That's a dangerous thing to do, what with the riffraff, the foreigners, and all. Any woman who does that—"

"I'm sorry, I really must say goodnight."

The landlady's pudding face turned red. "You'd better start looking for another apartment. Your lease is up on Sunday, and my son is already here. My place is too small for the both of us."

"I'll see what I can do. Now please, if you don't mind."

"Very well. Goodnight," Frau Pouls said abruptly and left, closing the door a little too hard.

꿍꿍꿍

The next morning, Amanda got on the phone to real estate firms. "I do have something suitable," one broker told her. "It will cost you twenty-five-hundred marks a month, plus two month's deposit up front."

"Is that the best you can do?"

"Where have you been, Frau Lee? There is a shortage of rentals, and my listings are the best available. Most people of quality prefer to buy."

"Okay, I'll take a look." This was going to be more difficult than Amanda had thought. She looked at dozens of apartments and found them all to be wanting. She even looked at rooms in private homes, but they lacked even a shred of privacy. At the end of a long search, the broker informed her that, for the kind of "luxury" she wanted, she'd have to buy, not rent, and that would also take time. Moving to a hotel was an option, but that was even more expensive, plus she'd have to pay storage for her personal things. When she finally got home late Saturday afternoon, she picked up the phone and dialed the number marked *private* on Wolf's card.

"Wolf Eichler here."

"I was afraid you might have gone away for the weekend."

"Amanda?"

"Yes."

"How are you?"

"Not so good. I've just spent days looking for an apartment."

"Any luck?"

"I'm afraid not. I have to be out by tomorrow. I should never have let something this important go so long."

"My offer of Marlene's condo still stands. I've already had a crew over there to put things in order. You can move in at any time.

"Well…"

"You would be doing me a great favor. I prefer someone be there rather than have it empty. Marlene considered you a good friend. She'd have wanted you to stay there."

"I still feel a little funny about it. I'm the one who found her."

"All traces of what happened are gone. But if you are uneasy in the master suite, you can close it off and use the guest room and bath."

"I don't know what to do." She couldn't move into any of the dumps she'd been shown—they were not only depressing, they were unsafe. At the same time, she didn't relish returning to the place where Marlene had died.

"You won't find something without searching for several weeks, maybe even months," Wolf said. "Is there someone you can stay with in the meantime?"

"No. I'd have to go to a hotel."

"I have a suggestion. Move into Marlene's condo and see how you feel. If you want to leave immediately, that's fine with me. I'll understand. At that point, you can go to a hotel if you prefer."

Amanda could think of no good alternative, and Wolf was being very generous. Maybe it would be okay. If Marlene's ghost haunted the place, it was a friendly ghost. "All right."

"Do you need someone to help you move?"

"I'm sure my assistant will help me. We can use the delivery van."

"Good. An excellent security system will be installed on Monday. Only you need to know the code. Meanwhile, I've left a set of the existing keys with Frau Kapps, the neighbor in number eighty-seven. I'm glad you've decided to move in."

∽∾∽

That night Amanda stayed up packing, using boxes from the local grocery store. She finished around two in the morning and was too hyper to sleep. She poured herself a glass of wine and looked around at the room, now denuded of all personal belongings.

If she hadn't met Marlene, she would have returned to New York, faced the music—as hard as that would have been—and gone back to being just another employee of a contemporary art gallery. Instead, she and Marlene had built a business that promised to be successful. How could she manage on her own? Amanda felt more

alone than she'd ever been in her life, only now the loneliness was tinged with fear and anxiety.

෬෩෬

At eleven o'clock on Sunday morning, Rolf pulled
up in the van. Less than half an hour later, they had loaded her ten or so boxes, paintings, and luggage. Traffic
was light as they headed out to Marlene's condo at Wagner Court. Amanda led the way in her car. The landlady's
son was glad to have the Ikea furniture and anything else
she didn't want.

Wolf had called Frau Kapps to let her know they
were coming. Vehicles were not allowed inside the
courtyard, except when people moved in or out or when
tradesmen performed services or made deliveries. Cars
for the residents were kept in a row of individual garages
just outside the electronic gate. Each one had a number
corresponding to its condo. Amanda parked the VW in a
space marked *Guests* then climbed into the front seat of
the van with Rolf. He was such a nice kid. She didn't
know what she'd do without him. Frau Kapps buzzed
them in, and they rolled up in front of number 85.

The smell of new paint greeted them as they entered.
Everything looked fresh and sparkling clean. It didn't
take them long to unload the van. Rolf stood by the door
ready to leave. "Are you sure you'll be okay here? Do
you want me to stay and help you unpack?"

She did want him to stay. She wasn't sure she'd be okay, but that was her problem, and Rolf had already given up most of his Sunday. "No, you go on. I'm sure you have a date waiting somewhere. Thanks for everything."

"See you tomorrow," he said and took off.

Not ready to face unpacking, she walked across the cobbled courtyard. She wanted to see if the Porsche was in the garage. Except for the cold wind whistling overhead, everything was quiet. People went out with their families on Sunday.

Number 85 had the garage at the end. She unlocked the door and looked in. There, glimmering like a jewel even in such dim light, was the Porsche. She ran her hand over the beautiful lines of the car from the back to the front. It had been Marlene's pride and joy. She'd ordered it as a divorce present for herself. This car was custom built. Marlene asked the manufacturer to match the paint to her favorite color of Chanel lipstick, Laque Rouge, a rich, almost ruby red.

"If I were to come back as a car," Marlene once said, "I would be a Porsche—low, sleek, and racy.'"

Amanda opened the door on the driver's side and slid in. The expensive leather seat cradled her body as she leaned back. She could smell faint traces of Marlene's perfume. *Why did she have to die and die so horribly? Who could have hated her that much?*

At the touch of a button, the cassette player began to play "*Du hast es gut.*" The melody was lilting, the lyrics ironic. The two of them used to laugh and sing along as they sped down the Autobahn. All of that was gone now. Gone forever. Once more, tears came to Amanda's eyes.

She opened the glove compartment, looking for a tissue, and she saw it. Thrown in toward the back was a tan snakeskin diary with the initials *M.E.*

❧❧

Dieter knocked on the door of Klaus Kruger's loft. European techno music boomed inside, spilling into the narrow hallway. There was no response. Annoyed, he pounded harder, trying to be heard.

"Go away," Kruger said.

"Open up. It's Dieter."

A red-eyed Kruger opened the door. His face was unshaven, and he wore only his green leather pants.

"My God, Klaus, you'll go deaf listening to that noise. Turn it off, please."

Kruger ambled over to his stereo and flipped a switch. The four-foot-tall speakers on either side of the loft fell silent. Dieter looked around for somewhere to sit down. There was only one folding chair leaning against the wall. The large space contained a mattress thrown on the floor with a soiled feather comforter tossed over the sheets. Canvases, an easel, and other artist's paraphernalia occupied the rest of the place. One wall and part of the ceiling were made of glass panes to maximize the light.

Dieter handed Klaus a check. "I came by to bring you this. It's your take from the show. I wrote it on my personal account so you wouldn't have to wait for your money." He unfolded the chair and sat down. "Amanda and I did very well by you and your exhibition."

Klaus plopped onto the mattress and sat cross-legged facing Dieter. "I think it is I who did well by you," he said. "After all, it is my art that's creating all the stir."

"Don't start believing your own press releases," Dieter said. "Remember, I'm the one who wrote them. Without my influence, no one would even glance at your work, and you know it. You owe it all to me, dear boy. Just a short time ago, you were selling fakes to tourists in Berlin. Your copies are still far better than your originals. After my television show next week, you'll be on your way. You'd be wise to stick to our agreement."

Kruger's black eyes narrowed, but he said nothing. Dieter got up to leave. "By the way, I advise you to lay off the drugs for a while. If you want to be a star, you must be reasonably presentable in polite society. You might consider buying another pair of pants. Those are disgusting."

Walking down the hallway, Dieter heard the techno music blasting once more from behind the door.

❦❦❦

Amanda headed back across the courtyard to the

condo. She went into the kitchen, put on a pot of coffee, and opened Marlene's appointment diary. Various episodes of her life were represented in pencil and colored ink. *Hair appointment with B,* obviously for Bauer. *Pick up dress from S* for Sophia. She came to the Thursday she had been mugged, two days before Marlene was killed. Penciled in for that evening was *Dinner with* followed by an initial again, written with Marlene's flourish. She'd had dinner with Hans Demuth that night. The initial must be an *H*.

For the next day, Friday, she had written, *Lunch at the Gemütlich Bier Halle with* and then an initial that could have been anything. It had just the slightest opening at the top. Could it be a K for Kruger? It was possible she had wanted to go over some details of the show with him, but she never mentioned it.

Under *Friday at midnight*, there was just a phone number, no initial or name. It was underlined several times so hard the pen had bitten into the paper. Amanda didn't recognize it. She picked up the kitchen phone and dialed the mystery number. It rang and rang, but there was no answer. She'd try again later.

Getting up to pour a cup of coffee, she noticed the door in the kitchen that led to the basement was ajar. That's where she'd asked Rolf to put the cartons of things she wouldn't need. She walked down the stairs. There was no way to enter the basement from outside except through one of the windows, and they were half-sized, closed, and locked. Rolf must have left the door open.

Back upstairs, Marlene's portrait smiled down on Amanda as she entered the living room. She was surprised to see a tall Lalique vase full of giant lavender tulips on the coffee table. There must have been at least two dozen. She picked up the card. *Welcome, Amanda. If there is anything you need, or you just want to talk, call me. Always, Wolf.* She could almost hear his voice saying the words. She dialed his number, and he answered right away.

"I just wanted to thank you for the lovely flowers. That was very thoughtful of you."

"They do brighten things up a bit. I hope you like tulips."

"One of my very favorites."

"Did my people leave the place presentable?"

"They did a beautiful job. I plan to keep Marlene's room closed off for now and just use the guest room."

"Poor Marlene," he said.

"She always wanted the two of you to get back together."

There was a long pause, then he said, "Marlene was a woman who ignored reality if it didn't fit into her plans. Although I was concerned for her welfare, any romantic feelings I had died a long time ago. I'll explain it to you someday."

"What time is the security system being installed?" Amanda asked.

"They'll be there tomorrow afternoon. I've requested that Frau Kapps let them in, so you don't have to take time from the gallery. Is that all right?"

"Yes."

"I'm going to Amsterdam tonight for an early morning meeting. We are hammering out the specifications for this new museum I'm designing, so I won't be back until late Tuesday afternoon," he said. "I was hoping we could have dinner that evening. There's a wonderful medieval restaurant in Aachen, about a forty-minute drive from Cologne."

"I'd like that."

"Good. I'll pick you up at eight."

Amanda felt a little happiness stir inside as she hung up the phone. She was surprised by how much she was looking forward to Tuesday.

New logs had been laid in the fireplace. She lit a fire, selected a book, and was settling in on the sofa when she heard a scratching noise. It was coming from behind the basement door. Then came a low and piteous meow. Amanda opened the door and in walked a black kitten with long fur and copper eyes.

"How did you get in here?" She'd checked earlier, and the windows were closed and locked. Turning on the single naked bulb, she went halfway down the stairs and saw that one of the windows was now open. Seeing no one, she walked over and slammed it shut. Probably the wind. The windows were hardly big enough for a man to crawl through. "How about something to eat?" she said to the cat. It was nice to have company, even if it was so small a being. "Tomorrow we'll see if you belong to anyone in the court."

Strange sounds and recent memories of Marlene caused Amanda to barely close her eyes as she tossed and turned in bed that night.

The next morning, she got up early. A ball of black fur was asleep at her feet. There was much to do today, including closing the Kruger sales and having Rolf deliver the paintings. He was working full time now. She also wanted to check out Hans Demuth and the unidentified number in Marlene's diary. She showered and dressed, then, with the cat at her heels, went downstairs and into the kitchen.

For a brief moment, she couldn't believe her eyes. When she realized what it was, she screamed. There on the kitchen table was a serrated knife with a long blade covered in blood.

CHAPTER 10

At seven o'clock Monday morning, Grutzmacher was already at his desk having a cup of black coffee. He was searching his pockets for a cigarette when Rudolf came in. "When did you get back?" Grutzmacher asked.

"Last night. It only took me two and a half hours from Amsterdam to Cologne by car." The unter kommissar sat across from his boss's desk and stretched out his long legs.

"What did you find out?"

"Well, as I suspected, Wolf Eichler's alibi is a little thin. His credit card was used to pay the bill at the Excelsior Restaurant around ten the night of the murder. Do you know how much a meal costs at that place? It's obscene. He did stay at the Hotel de L'Europe. I questioned the concierge, but he couldn't verify Eichler's comings and goings. There was a medical convention, and the hotel was packed."

"What about the airline?"

"Lufthansa confirmed he flew up on Friday night and back on Tuesday morning. That doesn't mean he couldn't have also made a round trip by car to murder his wife," Rudolph said.

"Did you check the car rental agencies?"

"Of course. I showed them his picture in case he used an alias. Nothing. But it would have been easy for him to leave his own car there from a previous trip. He frequently goes there on business. I think he's our man."

"He's certainly a possibility, but there are other suspects. The victim's last known lover, Hans Demuth, for one. He's married to that society woman who inherited the Vogt Steel fortune. Marlene and Herr Demuth were seen having a dinner the Thursday before she was killed."

Rudolf casually perused the statement obtained from the Klimt's waiter. "And according to Frau Lee, he threatened her in a phone call later," Grutzmacher said.

"Does he have an alibi?"

"He says he was at home with his wife all of Saturday evening. She backed him up."

"Well, there you are," Rudolf said.

"Not quite. If she forgave him for having an affair, she may lie to protect him."

"What about the servants?"

"They have Saturday nights and Sundays off,"

Grutzmacher said. "The neighbors on the right saw nothing, and the neighbors on the left, Herr and Frau Neef, are on holiday. Apparently, they took off the Sunday morning after the murder. They are due back tomorrow. I want you to call on them."

"I still think our killer is Eichler or that American woman, maybe both in collusion," Rudolf said.

"Thinking and proving are two different things. Meanwhile, we have to follow up every lead to get at the truth." Grutzmacher found it irritating the way Rudolf made up his mind then tried to ignore any other possibility. Perhaps he'd been trained this way at the Stasi in East Germany, but this type of thinking was not acceptable here. Grutzmacher savored the last drag off his cigarette and stubbed it out. "What's happening with the death painting?"

"Dieter Becker says it's very difficult to determine the identity of the artist since he is not using his own style. Still, Becker is checking all of his sources," Rudolf said.

"Have you spoken to the artists represented by the Lee Eichler Gallery?"

"We've checked them all out, and they are clean. Every one we interviewed had an alibi and was not personally involved with Marlene Eichler or Amanda Lee."

"When does Becker think he'll have something?"

"He hopes it will be soon."

"Well, we have to do more than hope," Grutzmacher

said. "Have a bit of the paint scraped off that canvas and analyzed. Then go to art supply stores and put together a list of the artists who use that type."

"That'll be every would-be painter in the city," Rudolf said. "Why not give Becker a little more time?"

"Just do it!"

ೞೞ

Amanda stood frozen in place. The knife in front of her must be the murder weapon. It was about fifteen inches long with a slightly curved, serrated blade and an ivory handle. Strands of blonde hair clung to the dried blood.

She dialed Grutzmacher's number. Her voice was shaking as she told him what had happened.

"I'll be right over," he said. "Don't touch anything and get out of the house in case he's still there."

Amanda threw on her coat and ran into the courtyard. Why did the murderer just leave the knife? Had he planned to harm her? Was he scared off by something? Did he even know she was there? To think he'd been in the condo a little before she came downstairs. By some grace of Fate, she had survived unscathed. After a few minutes, her heart reestablished its normal rhythm.

Grutzmacher and Rudolf arrived first, then the crime scene unit came. Amanda followed them back inside.

"Every bit of this place and the surroundings were

searched, and *you* find the murder weapon? Just what are you doing here anyway?" Rudolf said.

"We can't be sure it's the murder weapon until that is confirmed by tests," Grutzmacher said quietly. "We need to get this to the lab right away. Would you take care of that, please, Unter Kommissar?"

Rudolf glared at Amanda, bagged the knife, and stalked out.

Grutzmacher looked around the entire condo and examined both doors. "Once again, no forced entry."

Amanda told him about the window blowing open. "I don't see how such a small window could be used as an entryway," she said.

"You'd be surprised," Grutzmacher said. "If you're going to stay here, you had better change the locks and have bars put on the basement windows."

"Have you made any progress in the investigation?" Amanda asked.

"We can't discuss an ongoing case. Goodbye, Frau Lee."

The CSU stayed behind to dust the entire kitchen, the hallway, the front door, and every other conceivable place that might yield a condemning fingerprint.

When the police had gone, Amanda remembered the kitten and did a quick search. Big copper eyes melting into amber stared at her from under the sofa. She pulled him out, fed him, and took him with her to see Frau Kapps. "We'll find out whom you belong to," she said.

The old woman opened the door and stared at the small animal. "It's only a cat," Amanda said. "I promise to hold him on my lap."

"Come in," Frau Kapps said.

"Wolf Eichler said that you would be admitting the security system people. Could you ask them to put protective bars over the basement windows?"

"It looks like you need them. I saw the police over there again this morning."

"Someone broke in," Amanda said.

"Obviously, you weren't hurt. Was anything stolen?"

"No."

"There has never been an incident of any kind in this court, that is before Frau Eichler moved in. Now you. There's no end to it. Even the house number is unlucky. Eighty-five. Eight plus five equals thirteen, you know. Very unlucky." Frau Kapps looked at the cat.

"I wanted to ask you about this little fellow. I found him last night and wondered if you knew who the owner might be," Amanda said.

"That cat has no owner. It came here the day Frau Eichler died and has been hanging around ever since. We have called Animal Control several times, but it always gets away. I'll call them now and have it picked up."

"No, don't do that," Amanda said.

"All strays must be reported. It's the law."

"He is no longer a stray. As of this moment, he has a home with me."

"You'll be sorry. Black cats are a bad omen, especially ones that show up after a violent death."

"On the contrary, I consider him to be good luck. See you this afternoon."

Before Amanda headed to work, she checked the phone directory for a vet and picked one located near the gallery. She dropped the cat off with instructions to give him a bath, his shots, and a complete checkup.

As Amanda walked into the office, the phone rang. It was Wolf. His voice sounded stressed. "Frau Kapps called and told me what happened. Thank God you weren't harmed. I should never have let you move in before the new security system was installed."

"I'm fine Wolf, please don't worry. Besides, the new system is being put in this afternoon."

Amanda spent the rest of the morning writing invoices for the Kruger paintings. She would feel much happier with the new exhibit by a young American, Gregg Reed, the first artist chosen entirely on her own. His paintings were humorous and done in clear, bright colors. The new works would be mounted as soon as they came in. Amanda would have to think of a tactful way to tell Dieter that she would not be part of another Kruger extravaganza, even if the first one had resulted in financial success.

It was late afternoon before she had time to concentrate on Marlene's appointment diary. She once again tried to decipher the strange initial next to the Altstadt address, gave up, and decided to start with the mystery number. The phone rang a long time, again with no answer. *Well*, she thought, *I'll just keep calling every hour or so until someone picks up.*

Amanda flipped back a page to Thursday. Again she stared at the penciled-in engagement *Dinner with* and a fancy initial *H* for Hans Demuth. Marlene had sold a painting to Demuth. Amanda pulled the file. *One Cristopin acrylic, 76 cm x 91 cm, title: Longings, sold to HD.* There was no bill of sale, just a deposit slip for DM 10,000 cash. She found Demuth's direct telephone number on Marlene's Roledex and dialed. After a few seconds, he came on the line.

"This is Amanda Lee of Lee Eichler Gallery. I have a few matters I am trying to clear up regarding a painting my late partner sold you."

"There is nothing to clear up. It's been paid for and delivered." His voice was cold and businesslike.

"Since this transaction took place just before Marlene's death, I'm afraid she didn't get around to filling out the proper tax forms. Could I see you for a few moments? Wednesday, perhaps?"

"I'm terribly busy for the next several weeks."

"The forms must be turned in along with a bill of sale by the end of the week. I'm afraid the government frowns on noncompliance."

"Very well. Tomorrow afternoon at three." He hung up.

The rest of the day flew by. It was almost four o'clock and time to pick up the cat. Amanda asked Rolf to lock up. When the vet handed her the little guy, she hardly recognized him. The luxuriant long black coat was groomed to show-cat perfection.

"What a beauty you turned out to be," Amanda said.

"He appears to be a purebred Persian. We've given him all of his shots and prepared a package containing proper food, litter, everything you'll need," he said. "Could we have his name for our records?"

"He doesn't have one as yet."

"We must have a name to complete our files. You may change it later if you like."

"Well…I'll call him Regen," she said. She liked his new name, the German word for rain.

When she arrived home, she pulled her VW into the guest parking lot. She wasn't ready to start driving the Porsche. Gathering up the cat and her packages, she stopped in to see Frau Kapps. The old woman handed Amanda one set of the new keys. "I'm sending the other set to Herr Eichler. After all, it is his property."

Iron bars installed on the basement windows were visible as she approached the condo. They looked impregnable. All of the new locks were industrial strength. As soon as she entered the condo, she keyed in her personal code. A few minutes later, the security company phoned and acknowledged that the setup had been successful. No one could get in, unless she let them in.

Amanda released Regen from his new carrier, kicked off her shoes, and headed for a sherry in the living room. Quite a difference from her cramped one-room efficiency or those dreadful rentals. Curling up on the sofa, she took in the beauty of the space. A wedge of fading sunlight came through the French doors and fell on Wolf's tulips, touching the lavender with gold. They had opened, and their large heads curved gracefully over the Lalique vase. It had been a long time since a man had sent her flowers. She couldn't wait to see him again.

"I hope you don't mind," she said aloud to the portrait of Marlene. The painted lips smiled back. "Somehow, I don't think you do."

She headed upstairs to take a long, relaxing bubble bath. As she came to Marlene's bedroom, she paused. She had to face it sometime, better sooner than later. She opened the door.

The room had been completely redone. Marlene's pink draperies and bedclothes had been removed. A new modern bed had replaced the ornate French one. Gray silks were used in abundance on the bed and on the windows, where they culminated in a luxurious swirl on new dove-gray carpeting. Even with these changes, there was still a strong presence of Marlene.

Amanda walked over to one of the twin closets, which took up an entire wall. Many garments had never been worn. The tags still dangled from their sleeves. The second closet held an array of delectable nightgowns with matching negligees—gossamer creations, sexy and romantic at the same time.

She remembered Marlene's last trip to Milan.

"Look, *leibling*," she had said, holding up the latest Italian creation. "Will I not look fabulous in this? And here, I bought a little something for you." She'd handed Amanda a small velvet box. "For taking care of the gallery alone while I was off shopping. And for being such a good friend."

It was an Italian bracelet of eighteen-karat gold. The clasp was the head of a unicorn. Its horn was made of African amethyst carved into a spiral that came to a point. Green tsavorites made up its eyes.

"This little fellow will remind you that life has its magical moments. Savor them."

"It's beautiful. I'll save it for special occasions," Amanda said.

"Each day is a special occasion, *liebling*. Put it on and keep it on."

Amanda had worn the bracelet everyday since. Looking at it now caused a sadness to settle over her like a cloak. Marlene was not there to talk to. She would not offer her funny, usually sound, advice ever again. As Amanda closed the closet doors, something soft brushed against her ankles. It was little Regen. Picking him up, she held his small warm body next to her face.

એએએ

Tuesday afternoon, Wolf Eichler picked up the car phone and dialed. "Amanda, my meeting in Amsterdam lasted an hour longer than I anticipated. I'm on my way, but I'm afraid I can't be there until nine o'clock. Is that all right? I trust you won't be famished by then."

"We could make it another time if you prefer," she said, hoping he would not make it another time.

"No, I really want to see you this evening. I've made a reservation at The Minnesinger Restaurant in Aachen for nine-thirty. I'll be by for you at—"

"Why don't you give me directions and I'll meet you there? You need not drive all the way out here just to pick me up."

"I don't like the thought of you driving alone at night," he said. "Especially after what's happened."

"Really, Wolf. I'm a big girl."

"But—"

"No buts. Just tell me how to get there."

᥯

Rudolf had made an appointment for eight o'clock in the evening with Herr and Frau Neef, Hans Demuth's next-door neighbors. He was fifteen minutes early, so he waited in the car. The neighborhood's posh homes made him aware once more of life's injustices. Why should these self-indulgent people have all the things he lacked? Every day he worked hard, putting in long hours. Why?

So ingrates like this could feel safe on their satin sheets at night.

At exactly eight o'clock, he rang the doorbell. An elderly maid in a crisp uniform ushered him into the library. "Herr and Frau Neef will join you in a moment. Please have a seat."

Instead, he walked the length of the spacious room with his hands behind his back. His eyes ran over the leather-bound books—many first editions—the London club chairs with lamps placed for reading, the oriental rugs, and antique paintings of English hunt scenes. *Expensive but tasteless*, he thought. What he could do with their money.

When he cracked this case, he'd push old Grutzmacher straight into retirement, and he'd call the shots. As a newly promoted kommissar, he'd get a healthy raise and the recognition he deserved. But any policeman, even top brass, made far less than these people paid in taxes. Catching sight of himself in a bull's-eye mirror, he smoothed his straight blond hair with both hands just as the Neefs entered the room. They introduced themselves, and Rudolf flashed his badge as a formality.

Herr Neef was a fit-looking man in his late fifties.

That tweed jacket and pipe are all part of his stupid infatuation with the English, Rudolf thought.

His wife was athletic looking with short hair and no makeup. Amazing how so many upper class women had faces like horses. Just back from holiday, they were both newly tanned. It had been a long time since Rudolf had been on vacation—too long.

"Would you like something to drink?" Herr Neef asked. "There is *Wiezembier* on tap. I have half a dozen kegs sent up from Munich each year during Oktoberfest to enjoy with special guests."

"That would be fine." He would be off duty soon, anyway, and why shouldn't he have some Wiezembier? He deserved it far more than the silly ass sitting across from him. Frau Neef left briefly to give instructions to the maid.

After a few minutes of forced conversation about the weather, Rudolf got out his pen and notebook. "As I mentioned on the telephone, we are making some routine inquiries about your neighbor, Hans Demuth. You said you saw him last Saturday night?" The beer arrived in chilled steins, and Rudolf took a deep swig.

Herr Neef raised his chin slightly. "Yes, we saw Hans that night under rather unpleasant circumstances."

"And what might those be?"

"We gave all this information to the police at the time, but I am glad to repeat it if it will help expedite matters."

Rudolf was somewhat taken aback. No one in his division had questioned these two. They'd already gone on vacation. "Please do," he said.

"That particular Saturday evening, my wife and I were coming home from the opera. It was well after mid-

night." He looked at Frau Neef, who nodded in agreement. "We had orchestra seats for the opening of *Die
Valkyrie*. As we were turning into our driveway, Demuth
collided with us, and we suffered damage to our new
Jaguar. Quite annoying."

"Did you have words with him?" Rudolf asked.

"I was about to, but when he got out of his car, I
could see there was a bit of blood on his shirt. I told him
he'd better go home, that we'd discuss the accident in the
morning."

"Was his nose bleeding or did he have a cut on his
head?"

"I couldn't tell. Frankly, it was quite dark, and I was
very upset over what he'd done to our car. Since Demuth
obviously could walk and talk, or rather curse, I assumed
his injuries to be superficial. We filed a report with the
police, all very proper for insurance purposes."

"So it was the traffic police you spoke to," Rudolf
said.

"Well, yes. The next morning, Hans stopped by for a
moment to discuss the incident. He seemed perfectly fine
then. Didn't mention any injuries, only how inconvenient
it would be to do without his car while it was in the
shop."

"Had Demuth been drinking that night?" Rudolf hated to let the privileged get away with any infraction of
the law.

"Perhaps. His behavior was completely obnoxious.

He actually tried to blame me for pulling in front of him. The fact is, I didn't see him. I believe his lights were out."

"Probably trying to sneak home so Helga wouldn't know when he got in," Frau Neef said. "I don't know why she puts up with that man."

"So she wasn't with him."

"Heavens no. He doesn't take her along on his tomcatting expeditions." Frau Neef shook her head. "He drives his silver BMW on those occasions. When they go out together, they always take the Mercedes."

Rudolf paused a moment, pen in hand, but didn't write anything. This little dustup complicated things. He'd thought he had this case all tied up in a neat little package with Eichler as the prime suspect.

"You aren't here to investigate our little accident, are you, sir?" Herr Neef said. "Is Demuth in some kind of trouble?"

The woman exchanged looks with her husband. "What has he done this time?"

CHAPTER 11

Amanda inched her way through the heart of medieval Aachen. Frost glittered like pavé diamonds on the narrow cobbled streets. Freezing temperatures and the late hour had left the area uninhabited by all but the ghosts of the Frankish kings. Their spirits seemed to linger in the shadows or peer down through ancient windows.

At last, she found Frankenstrasse, and the atmosphere changed completely. Expensive cars were parked bumper to bumper on both sides of the brightly lit street near the castle and restaurant. There was barely enough room to squeeze by, and the nearest parking place was two blocks away. She managed to tuck the VW into a tight space and gave herself a quick check in the mirror.

As she entered the Minnesinger, she stepped into a different world. A lute was playing softly, creating a pleasant background for dinner conversations. The place was large but somehow intimate, with centuries-old stone walls and a fireplace big enough for a man to stand in. Burning logs and flickering candles added to the romantic setting. The maître d' greeted her with a small bow.

"I'm Amanda Lee. I'm meeting—"

"Follow me," he said. "Herr Eichler is waiting for you." He led her up a flight of stairs to one of several small balconies that jutted out over the room below.

Wolf rose to greet her.

"Would you like the champagne now, sir?"

Wolf nodded, and the maître d' disappeared. For a few moments, neither said anything, but the silence was not awkward. It seemed natural that they were here together in this beautiful place.

"Do you like it?" he asked.

"I love it." The romantic atmosphere, the presence of Wolf—it all had a dreamlike quality.

"I haven't been here in a long while, but I consider it a special place," he said.

The delicate sound of the lute drifted up from below, and a youth began to sing in Old German.

"He's singing about ancient times, when the knight-poets or minnesingers wandered from castle to castle with verses of praise for the beauty of ladies and the honor of knighthood."

As he took her hand, his clear blue eyes studied her hair, the features of her face, her mouth. She could not yet read the secrets behind those eyes. She saw only their blueness, their intensity. The waiter arrived and presented the wine for Wolf's approval, then poured it into golden chalices.

"Where in the States are you from?" Wolf asked.

"Originally from Virginia."

He raised his glass. "To Virginia. It must be a fascinating place to produce such an extraordinary young woman."

"I'm not extraordinary," she said, meaning it.

"Oh, but you are. You have a sensitivity, a genuineness, and a humility rare in a beautiful woman."

She gave him a small, slightly embarrassed smile. "How did you come to that conclusion? You barely know me."

"It's quite evident." He squeezed her hand then released it as the waiter approached with menus.

The oversized *Speisekarten* were beautifully handwritten in script. There was a red wax seal with a crown insignia at the bottom.

For hours they discussed art, architecture, something of her recent life in New York, his life in Düsseldorf—exploring each other, peeling back those first fragile layers of thoughts, hopes, and dreams.

"You have a lot of courage," he said.

The waiter unobtrusively removed the dinner dishes and served the coffee.

"What do you mean?"

"Living in a foreign country, operating a business here, sticking to it even after what's happened. All on your own."

"It seems that I've always been on my own."

He smiled. "I'm sure it's not from lack of admirers."

It was no wonder Marlene had spent the last year of her life trying to win him back. Looking at the restaurant below, Amanda could see it was almost empty. The waiters were preparing to close.

How long will he find me appealing before he moves on to someone else? A week, a month, six months? The disaster with Karl flashed through her mind. Old insecurities began to arrive like unwanted, quarrelsome relatives.

"Is something wrong?" Wolf said.

"I was just thinking how late it must be, and there's still the drive home."

"Yes, of course." He signaled for the check. "You must be tired. I'm sorry; I should have realized."

Leaving the Minnesinger, they were greeted by softly falling snow. A white blanket of several inches covered the ground. He put his arm around her, and they headed for her car. "No matter what you say," he said, "I'm following you home."

They reached the VW, and he brushed off the windshield. As he held the door, she slid into the icy interior. Coughing and whining, the engine refused to turn over. "Sometimes it takes a few tries," she said.

After several minutes, it still wouldn't start.

"Come, leave this here. I'll send someone for it to-morrow."

Soon they were in his large warm Mercedes, heading for Cologne. The cold and the snow had turned everything into a blue-white dreamscape complete with crystal trees. Wolf reached over and took her hand. The gesture stirred strong feelings of pleasure mixed with reservation. Other men in her life had come and gone, but this one could hurt her far more than she cared to endure.

When they reached the condo complex, the snow had stopped, and stars twinkled overhead.

"You need only see me to the gate." The key was already in her hand. "Goodnight, Wolf. Thank you for a wonderful evening."

Before she could escape into the courtyard, he took her in his arms, and she felt the soft fabric of his topcoat against her cheek. Then he lifted her chin and kissed her forehead, her eyelids, her nose, and, finally, her lips with a gentleness that hinted of restrained passion.

CHAPTER 12

With eyes puffy from sleep, Helga Demuth propped herself up on large fluffy pillows and reached for the breakfast tray next to the bed. As she did most mornings, she munched a sweet roll and watched her husband get ready for work. Coming out of the bathroom fresh from his shower, he toweled off drops of water still clinging to his taught, slender body.

She envied his slimness. The best spas in Europe had failed to remove the love handles from her waist or the bulges from her hips for any length of time. Recently, she'd given up trying. "What's on for today, Hans?" she asked as he slapped on expensive French cologne.

"This morning I'm meeting with Gustof to discuss equipment for the new Essen foundry. After that, I thought I'd take him to lunch at Die Glocken."

"And this afternoon?"

Seemingly absorbed in combing his hair, he avoided her eyes in the mirror. "And this afternoon?"

She'd know if he was telling her the truth. His secretary was on her payroll, as was the private detective she'd just hired. Of course, Hans knew nothing of him.

"I have an appointment with that American woman," he said touching up his mustache.

"What American woman?" She tried not to let anxiety slip into her voice.

"You met her at the Lee Eichler Gallery the night of the Kruger exhibition."

Marlene Eichler was still a sore subject. Just hearing her name gave Helga a headache. Was her partner to be the next threat? "What does she want?"

He slipped into his shirt and came over to have her knot his tie. "Come *schatz*, don't start. I've learned my lesson, believe me." He kissed her cheek. "She simply wants some tax information for a painting I bought for our new building. It's a nuisance, but I have to see her."

"I'm warning you, Hans, I will not tolerate another affair. One more and I'll throw you out." Memories of the humiliation, the tears, the sleepless nights attacked her mind like a swarm of bees.

"Helga, really. You know there's no one else. Marlene was a bad mistake, I admit it. But she's gone—for good. I've got to run. Call you later." Grabbing his jacket, he blew her another kiss and retreated through the bedroom door.

Although Helga had lied to the police to give him an alibi, she still had the shirt he'd worn the night Marlene was murdered. It had a splatter of blood on the front, and she was fairly certain it was not his. She'd have noticed any cuts or scratches. Like a fool, he'd simply tossed it into the laundry with everything else. The maid had brought it to her attention.

That shirt was now in a safe place, and should he cheat again, she'd send it straight to the police. If it was Marlene's blood, the justice system would take care of Hans, and she wouldn't have to spend a cent. In any case, Hans was skating on thin ice.

Marlene was not his first affair. She knew that. He'd been cheating from the beginning, but he'd always been discreet. As long as he didn't flaunt the fact, she could tolerate it, even fool herself that it wasn't happening. Then came Marlene. He was positively careless, and all of their friends seemed to know. She stuffed another sweet roll into her mouth.

* споз*

Reading the latest report from forensics, Grutzmacher was not surprised to learn there were no fingerprints on the knife found by Frau Lee. The blood and hair matched those of the victim, which he'd also expected. The weapon itself, however, could still prove helpful. It had been identified as a South African hunting knife that dated back to the turn of the nineteenth century, a real collector's item. Photographs were being distributed to all antique weapons dealers.

Rudolf's conversation with Herr and Frau Neef had also been most interesting. They certainly validated Demuth as a suspect, even though Rudolf insisted at every opportunity that the real killer was Wolf Eichler.

The analysis of the paint used in the death painting would be done soon. They had taken tiny scrapings from several areas of the painting now facing the wall. Grutzmacher got up and turned it around to try to look once more into the mind of the killer. Why had the style of Edward Hopper been chosen? Why did the murderer paint it—or have it painted—at all? If it had been done as a souvenir of his act, why did he, or she for that matter, leave it behind to be discovered? The questions were obvious, the answers illusive.

⌘⌘

Sleeping in was a rarity for Amanda, but this morning it was just too tempting. As she snuggled down between the smooth cotton sheets, she went over every delicious detail of her evening with Wolf—the play of candlelight on his face, his eyes, the gentle sensuality of their first kiss. They had parted at the gate, as she requested, and he'd stood watch until she was safely inside the condo. Reluctantly, she got out of bed and into the shower.

The warm water felt wonderful as it splashed over her body.

It would be so nice to have a normal life again, to be free to come and go, free to run her business, free to have a relationship, free to just walk down the street without constantly looking for enemies in every shadow.

That couldn't happen until Marlene's killer was caught. As far as Amanda knew, the police weren't making great progress, and they certainly weren't sympathetic to her. In fact, they viewed her as a possible suspect. No, it was time to stop being a victim and start trying to find out who murdered Marlene.

She had an appointment with Hans Demuth this afternoon. Perhaps this meeting would reveal something of interest. Amanda remembered meeting Demuth and his wife at the Kruger opening. Today, at three o'clock, she'd have her chance to get an up-close look at Herr Demuth.

She decided on a gray suit with a pencil skirt and pearl earrings. Her watch and the unicorn bracelet were her only other accessories. Little Regen scampered around her feet as she got ready to leave. Amanda picked him up and gave him a farewell hug. "Wish me luck today," she said.

He responded with a low purr.

Last night's snow crunched beneath her feet as she headed for her garage. Since the VW had zonked out last night, she'd have to take the Porsche. She slid into the rich leather interior and put the key into the ignition. No one had driven this car but Marlene. She'd treated it like a living entity, talking to it as she flew down the Autobahn, praising it as she passed virtually everything on the road. As Amanda turned the key, she half expected the Porsche to rebel against a strange hand, like a loyal steed in a sentimental Western movie. Instead, the car started on the first try.

Rolf had already opened the gallery when she arrived. Her assistant had turned out to be a real treasure. He was barely out of college, and this was his first job. Pouring her a cup of coffee, he gave a low whistle as she took off her coat.

"Shouldn't you show a little more respect for your employer?"

"As you wish, *meine dame*," he said with exaggerated formality, and they both burst out laughing. "By the way, somebody called about your VW. They said it wasn't worth fixing."

"My poor little bug. I will miss it. But not too much."

As Amanda and Rolf walked the length of the gallery, they discussed the upcoming Gregg Reed show.

"What will Herr Becker say when he finds out about this?" Rolf asked.

"Hopefully, he'll be his usual gracious self. He surely doesn't expect to choose our artists forever. That was just till we got our sea legs."

Rolf rolled his eyes heavenward. "Right."

"Don't send out the invitations to the show until I've had a chance to speak to him."

He gave her a salute.

She went into her office and dialed Dieter's number. "I wanted to invite you over to preview our next show. The paintings arrive tomorrow."

"You have a new show planned already? Who is the artist, my dear? I don't recall our discussing anyone. I rather thought you'd leave the Kruger works on display for a while."

"The Krugers have been shipped out," she said. "I've chosen an American, Gregg Reed. He's quite good; I think you'll like him."

There was a long pause. "I thought we always made these decisions together."

"Dieter, you've been most generous with your time and expertise, but I've got to try my own wings. I'd like you to see Reed's work. He's been very well received in New York. Perhaps we could—"

Click. The silence was like a chill in the air. *Well,* she thought, *I'm sure he'll get over it. He'll have to.*

Rolf came in carrying an armload of purple and lavender flowers wrapped in cellophane and ribbon. There were irises, tulips, freesia, and several varieties she'd never seen before.

"They're beautiful, where did they come from?"

"You tell me," he said as he handed her a small white envelope. "I hope we have a vase big enough."

She opened the card. *My darling Amanda. Thank you for a most memorable evening. These flowers reminded me of the scent of your hair. Wolf.*

დასდ

At three p.m. sharp, Amanda arrived at Hans Demuth's suite in the Vogt Steel Tower and was greeted by his secretary. A few moments later, she was ushered into his office. The furnishings were superbly designed in what was obviously polished Vogt steel. The upholstery and general color scheme were in soft neutral tones to set off the large Kandinsky dominating the wall. Amanda hadn't seen anything like it outside of a museum. Hans Demuth came from around his paper-free desk to greet her. His mood was infinitely more pleasant today than it had been on the phone.

"Good afternoon, Frau Lee. Impressive, is it not? It was painted in the early 1900s, during Kandinsky's years in Munich."

"It looks as if it could be part of his *Composition* series. Supposedly three of the ten *Compositions* were lost during the war," she said.

"So I've heard." His mustache stuck out a little at the edges like the whiskers of a carnivorous animal. "I like this particular work because of the dramatic use of black." Demuth indicated that she sit on the sofa. He took the chair next to her. He headed a major steel company, enjoyed every luxury, and moved in top social circles—all through the largess of his wife. "Would you like some coffee or perhaps a drink?"

"No thanks."

"Well then, what can I do for you?"

"I need your help in filling out these papers. My partner didn't record her transaction with you, and I must figure the taxes. Could you confirm how much you paid for the work?"

"It wasn't very much. Around ten thousand marks cash. I could have told you that over the phone." He smiled, but his eyes did not.

"I also need your signature on this bill of sale—here." She indicated a line at the bottom of the page. "I'm sorry to bother you. It was unlike Marlene to forget something like this."

"As I recall, she had other things on her mind that night." He moved next to her on the sofa, took out a gold Mont Blanc pen, and signed his name with an assured hand. A whiff of his cologne floated in her direction. It was sweet and cloying.

"My relationship with your partner ended rather badly. But then I'm sure she must have told you all about it."

"I only remember that she had dinner with you the Thursday before she died." Amanda watched his face, trying to read some emotion, but his features didn't change.

"Mmmm, I believe it was. Marlene was not a woman

of discretion, you know, and that is very important to a man in my position."

"I can see how it would be."

"And what about you? Are you a woman of discretion?"

Amanda didn't reply. She gave one copy of the bill of sale to Demuth and put the other one in her purse.

"Yes," he said, answering his own question. "You seem much more sensible. As it happens, Frau Lee, I need several large contemporary paintings for the offices of our new foundry in Essen. Do you have anything that I might find of interest?"

Amanda was somewhat taken aback. "Well, yes, we do have a few new things, but—"

"Would you agree to give me a private showing?" His eyes crawled down her body.

"I'm very busy at the moment, getting ready for a new show." She hoped the light tone in her voice hid the discomfort beginning to churn in her stomach.

"Galleries are always looking to make sales. That's why you are in business, yes?" He'd moved uncomfortably close.

She stood up. "You're welcome to come by any time you like. We are open from ten to six. I must be going. I have another appointment in half an hour."

He smiled. "Of course. However, during the day it is difficult for me to get away. I'll come by tonight, say at eight o'clock? I look forward to seeing you then."

CHAPTER 13

Once outside the Vogt Steel Tower, she hurried along the busy street toward her car. The crowd was normal for this time of day, yet she felt like a crushing horde was pushing her along. The cold air was not responsible for the chill that seemed to penetrate her bones.

Amanda hadn't expected Hans Demuth to respond as he had. She had mixed feelings about the whole encounter. The thought of being alone with him was unsettling. Still, she might find out more about his relationship with Marlene.

When she got back to the gallery, she asked Rolf to join her in the back room. "We must pull out some of the larger and more expensive pieces."

"For which client?" Rolf asked.

"Hans Demuth."

Rolf gave a low whistle. "Herr Vogt Steel. That's major money."

When they'd finished making their selections, they arranged the paintings along a shelf for easy viewing. Amanda asked Rolf if he could come back at nine o'clock.

"If you want me here," he said, "I'll be here."

Thank God, she thought.

෧෧෧

Amanda grabbed dinner at a nearby café. At seven-forty p.m., she parked the Porsche in its spot in front of the gallery. When she turned off the ignition, a misty rain covered the windshield like fairy dust. She remembered the night she was mugged. That had marked the beginning of her private hell. She glanced quickly around the parking lot. No one was there. Before getting out of the car, she found the keys to the gallery in her bag then ran the few steps to the front door.

Flipping on the lights in her office, she noticed the answering machine blinking. Before she could push the *messages* button, a car turned into the parking lot, its headlights flooding the windows. Hans Demuth, fifteen minutes early!

The night bell announced her visitor. She reluctantly went to the door. He stood there grinning, a silver bucket with ice and champagne under one arm.

She unlocked the door and let him in. "Good evening, Herr Demuth."

"Call me Hans." He held up the champagne. "Looking at art is thirsty work." He followed her into the office, where she took his topcoat and scarf. She was surprised to see he had on a dinner jacket.

While he opened the champagne, she took down crystal flutes. Maybe a glass of wine would drown some of the butterflies fluttering against the walls of her stomach. He touched his glass to hers.

"To art," he toasted. "Well, lovely lady, what do you have for me?"

๛๛๛

Rolf sat on a bed in the emergency room at Kölner Krankenhaus, pain shooting through his left shoulder. He hoped Amanda had gotten his message. "Damn rain—my bike was totaled," he told the young intern who was patching him up.

"You were lucky, my man. You could've been totaled," the intern said.

๛๛๛

Amanda stood by the last of the paintings. The way Demuth looked at her instead of the canvases made her cringe.

She surreptitiously glanced at her watch. Nine o'clock.

"I thought you would particularly like this work," she said. "It's by Cristopin, the same artist who did the work Marlene sold you."

Hans sat on the small sofa across from Amanda as she presented the painting. The champagne had been placed on a coffee table in front of him. He had consumed almost the entire bottle of wine by himself and was beginning to show the effects.

"By the way, where did you meet Marlene?" Amanda said.

"Just where you'd expect, in a bar."

"Which one?"

"What difference does it make?"

"None. I was just curious about how you met and how long you'd know her, that's all."

"I only knew her a few months." His gaze shifted from her to the painting. "This is quite good."

"Yes. Marlene discovered him. She predicted his career would take off in a year or so."

"Possibly." He downed the wine in his glass. "I'm very rich, you know. I'll take all of these if it will make you happy."

"You should buy what makes you happy." He put down his glass and moved toward her. "Is there any wine left?" Amanda said.

Demuth went back to the table and pulled the green

bottle out of melting ice. There was just another half glass each. Moving in very close, he handed a glass to Amanda. She backed away slightly and took a sip.

Hans began running his finger up and down her arm. He put down his glass and ran his hand along her back. His closeness mixed with the champagne almost made her sick.

She gently pushed him away. "Stop, please."

"I see that you and Marlene are very much alike when it comes to playing games," he whispered, his groping hand fumbling for her breast.

Her revulsion was exceeded only by her anger.

His other hand was moving under her skirt, sliding up between her thighs. "You tease and then reject."

He was no longer smiling. His breaths grew quick and shallow as he pinned her against the wall and ground into her with his lower body. She was gripped by panic and pleaded with wordless sounds. Her face turned from side to side as if trying to deny the reality of the assault.

"Stop pretending you don't want me. You're the type who likes it rough. Just feel me," he said, forcing her free hand down to his groin.

Incredibly, he seemed to think that engaging in forcible rape was somehow a tribute to her sex appeal and that she should be flattered.

When he drew back to see her reaction, she threw her champagne in his face. For a moment he stopped cold. Drops of wine clung to his lashes and ran down his cheeks. He took out a handkerchief and slowly wiped his face.

He grabbed her, forcing his mouth hard against hers. She bit him on the lip. He yelled in pain and surprise. As he raised his fist to hit her, there was a loud crash just outside the window. Demuth looked up. Whatever he saw through the half open blind caused him to run from the room. A few seconds later, she heard the front door open and a car roar away. Amanda peered through the window. She saw a man in a dark hat and coat hurry across the street and get into an old Audi.

CHAPTER 14

After locking the front door, Amanda went into her office and collapsed on the sofa. Who was the man in the Audi? Thank God for him, whoever he was.

The blinking light on the answering machine caught her eye. She pushed the button and heard Rolf say he'd been in an accident. She called the hospital and finally reached him at his rooming house.

Rolf went through a brief description of his eventful evening. "Don't worry, boss, my landlady's taking good care of me. Sorry I wasn't there for you. What happened?"

"Nothing, Rolf. Stay out as long as you need to," Amanda said. "I'll check on you tomorrow."

❧❧

At nine-thirty Thursday morning, Wolf Eichler stopped working on plans for the Amsterdam museum and closed his eyes. Amanda's face entered his mind, and he could almost hear her laughter.

Although she bore a striking resemblance to Marlene physically, she was completely different in every other way. She had a softness, a sweetness he found irresistible.

The intercom buzzed, startling him into the here and now. "Herr Eichler," Frau Witt's voice boomed, "there's someone here from the Cologne police. Unter Kommissar Rudolf."

"Show him in," Wolf said, and Rudolph appeared at the door.

"Please have a seat. Is this about Marlene?" Wolf was eager for news that this nightmare might soon be over so that he and Amanda could move on with their lives.

"Do you recognize this?" Rudolf leaned over the desk and dropped the distinctive lapis stud into Wolf's palm.

"My God. It looks like it's from a set I bought at auction a few months ago. Where did you get this?"

"It was found in your ex-wife's bedroom on the occasion of her death. It took us quite a while to trace it to you. Do you know how it got there?"

"I honestly don't." Wolf stared at the antique stud. He could feel Rudolf watching him. "The last time I saw it was the day I brought the set home and placed it in the top drawer of my dresser."

"Who else has access to your place?"

"Only the cleaning lady. She's been with me for over two years. I don't think she would ever take anything."

"What is her name?"

"Markrit Algar."

"An immigrant?"

"Yes. She's from Turkey."

"Her address?"

"She lives at Münsterplatz. Number forty-five."

Rudolf scribbled the information in his notebook. "Have you had any break-ins or robberies lately?"

"Not to my knowledge, although obviously, someone took this stud."

"Do you have a security system, Herr Eichler?"

"Of course. I have many valuable works of art and antiques."

"I see. Forgive me, but I must ask. Did you leave this stud in your ex-wife's bedroom the night she was murdered?"

"Absolutely not," Wolf said. "I had no reason to kill Marlene, and I've been over my whereabouts for that night."

Rudolf plucked the stud from Wolf's hand. "I'll just take this. Evidence, you know. We may have further questions."

"Should I contact my advocate?"

"Good day, Herr Eichler." Rudolf turned and strode through the door, leaving it open.

Frau Witt looked in, obviously curious, but quietly closed the door.

Wolf realized his hands were trembling. How did that stud get from his dresser drawer to Marlene's bedroom? The nightmare was not over. The worst was yet to come.

 දුරුදුරු

The dom's clock struck ten a.m., its ancient bells chiming musically throughout Cologne. A weak ray of sunlight began to melt the frost on the window of the Trella Boutique. Sophia Danielle looked critically at her handiwork. The red Valentino dress was the perfect choice. It was sure to attract wealthy clients for the coming holidays. She placed a matching beaded bag in the mannequin's hand and climbed down from the display.

This was where she loved to be, surrounded by beautiful things. She enjoyed the changing seasons. Each season brought in a whole new batch of the lovely designs she personally selected from Milan, Paris, and Düsseldorf. It was her good taste that made the important women in this town appear so well turned out. Many of them wouldn't set foot outside their doors without her telling them what to wear. She was a very successful woman, and she'd done it all on her own.

Sophia took a sip of steaming black espresso and surveyed her newly decorated domain. It had cost a lot of money, but it was worth it. The interior designer had gotten rid of all the fake Louis XVI pieces and replaced them with authentic Art Deco. He said that it suited her because she looked rather Deco herself. Tall and slim, she had almost no bosom or hips. Her sleek, dark hair was worn in a short bob. "This style is a perfect match to your own," he said.

She agreed completely and loved the end result.

Two burled elm wardrobes, designed by Èmile-Jacques Ruhlmann in the late 1920s, held the designer collections. Display cases made of the same wood in a similar style showed off jewelry and accessories. In a small recessed sitting area, Clément Mère armchairs, upholstered in green leather, stood out against an ecru wall.

The only thing left from before the redesign of the boutique was a painting she'd purchased some time ago. It used to sit in the back dressing room on the floor, unframed and unnoticed. She had already put it with the trash when the interior designer saw it. He liked the bold colors and the subject, a lone woman looking out of a window. "It is very reminiscent of Edward Hopper, and works well in this space. We'll keep it." He then sent it out to be framed in expensive lacquered wood.

The total effect of the new décor was impressive. Today, she had to do some billing to help pay for it. In the back room, Sophia brought up Accounts on her computer. Frau Beton only owed DM 900, Frau Classen, DM 1,500. Frau Demuth owed her over DM 20,000. Poor Helga. The most beautiful clothes in the world couldn't do much for that figure. When she looked under *E*, she was surprised to see that Marlene Eichler still owed her for a black silk Chanel. She'd died, leaving an unpaid balance of DM 3,000. Sophia was not going to get stuck for that amount. Her business partner would just have to pay it. Printing out a bill, she marked it to the attention of Amanda Lee at the Lee Eichler Gallery.

༻ↀↀↂ༺

Humming a happy little tune, Markrit Algar admired her new hat. It was bright blue felt with a colorful feather. She'd make a nice impression on her son and his friends when she arrived in Munich. Spending her vacation with him would be wonderful. She adjusted the hat this way and that over her still-pretty face. It had come from one of the finer shops in Düsseldorf. True, she'd splurged a little, but she wanted her boy to be proud of her. All her life she'd worked hard for enough to raise her child, and she was finally making sufficient money to afford a few extras. Things were much better for her in Germany than they'd ever been in Turkey.

She liked Herr Eichler. He was always so kind and quite generous. Lucky for her, she had been the one se-lected as his housekeeper over many others. *Look at the time!* She should have left five minutes ago to comfortably catch the train. Now she'd have to rush.

As she closed her suitcase, she heard the doorbell.

Who could that be? Her neighbors kept to themselves, and she wasn't expecting anyone. Well, whoever it was would just have to understand that she had no time to be sociable. She hurried down the narrow hall of the small basement flat and opened the door. She was surprised to see the telephone service man. He'd stopped by Herr Eichler's several days ago to upgrade the service. She had not been aware that there was anything wrong with it, but she'd let him in to do his work. Funny, he wasn't wearing his uniform.

"Good morning sir. I don't need any changes in my telephone service, at least not now. I'm on my way to catch a train."

He said nothing, but came in and closed the door behind him.

"Sir, I don't think you understand."

An expression crossed his face that frightened Markrit. Her dark eyes widened as he reached into his coat pocket and pulled out a gun with a silencer attached. Screaming, she turned and ran into the bedroom and tried to close the door. He easily pushed it open, knocking her down.

She felt a burning explosion in her shoulder. "Please sir, don't kill me. I've nothing of value. Why would you want to—"

He shot her again, this time in the knee. The hollow-point nine-millimeter bullet spread open like a flower on impact rather than passing through her leg. Blood gushed from her knee. With great effort, she dragged herself toward the phone on the nightstand. Her hand had just reached the receiver when she felt another bullet rip into her upper back. Blood poured from her wounds, soaking into the carpet. She moaned and fell against the side of the bed. Her poor son. He'd be all alone.

ფოფ

The gallery felt empty without Rolf. Amanda spent the day planning the Reed exhibition. Several times she dialed the mystery number in Marlene's diary, but no one answered. Only one or two people came into the gallery, and they were "just looking," so she closed early and went home.

Later that evening, she decided to try the number again. Maybe she'd get lucky this time. The phone rang and rang. As she was about to hang up, a gruff voice said, "Chez Otto." She could hear loud laughter and drunken singing in the background.

"Is this six, two, one, nine, two, two, eight?"

"That's right. Who'd you want to speak to?"

"Uh…let me speak to Otto."

"You a friend of his?"

"Yes." She waited for several minutes.

The same gruff voice came back on the line, almost shouting to be heard over the background noise. "Otto's gone out. He'll be back in an hour or so. It's hard to speak on the phone here. If you want to talk to him, why don't you come by around eleven-thirty?"

"I forget where you are located," Amanda said.

He gave her an address on the other side of Cologne, in an area unfamiliar to her.

❧❧❧

The sleek Porsche made its way down a gaudy strip illuminated by neon. According to the instructions Amanda had been given on the phone, she was only a few blocks away from her destination. A handful of prostitutes were clustered near the corner, braving the damp night in stiletto heels, flimsy dresses, and cheap furs. The expensive car drew their attention, and two of them started toward Amanda making obscene gestures. She speeded up and left them behind. *You must be crazy*, she told herself. *Turn around*. But she kept going. This place had been important to Marlene the Friday before she died. It might help to know why.

She located the address on a narrow side street. Hanging over a dingy glass door hung a sign which said, Chez Otto. A frigid rain began to fall, and the street was completely empty. Amanda sat in the car for a few moments, screwing up her courage, then got out and headed for the entrance. As she reached the door, it swung open, and a big man who looked like a wrestler bid her welcome. She recognized the gruff voice. "I've come to see Otto," she yelled over the din coming from the room behind them.

"You the one who called?"

"Yes."

"Follow me." The bouncer led her from the small dark corridor into what appeared to be a late night cabaret. There was a stage with a microphone, a few abandoned musical instruments, and a cheap backdrop of naked female silhouettes. Tables were clustered around the stage, occupied mostly by men and a dozen or so women. A thick haze hung in the air that reeked of stale smoke, beer, and heavy perfume. Amanda could almost feel her hair and clothes absorbing the offensive odors.

On the opposite side of the room was a long, crowded bar without stools. Some of the patrons leaning against its brass railing eyed her as she passed by and broke out into a chorus of drunken catcalls, hooting, and shrill laughter. The gruff-voiced man took her arm and propelled her through the crowd. He stopped at a table in the back of the room where a man was sitting alone, his face in shadow.

"Otto, this is your friend what called." The bouncer pulled out a chair and pushed it under Amanda's legs so forcefully she landed in the seat with a thud. She looked across the table.

Otto was completely bald with a thick neck. On one of his fingers, he wore a diamond ring. The stone flashed as he reached for a cigar. He had on a custom-made tuxedo, but even its exquisite cut and luxurious fabric couldn't add the slightest touch of class to the man wearing it. He sat staring at Amanda with dull brown eyes. The look made her uncomfortable, but she stared back.

Finally, he said, "To what do I owe this pleasure?"

"I understand that my business partner, Marlene Eichler, visited your club. In fact, she was here the night before she died."

"Lots of people come here."

"I was hoping you could tell me something about that evening—who she was with, who she spoke to."

"And why should I do that?"

"She was a dear friend and—any information you can give me would be appreciated."

Otto signaled a waiter and ordered a bottle of champagne. "What's the matter, you don't trust Grutzmacher and his band of merry men?"

"Perhaps."

As the waiter put a glass before her, she noticed an old lipstick print smudged along the top. Otto noticed it too.

"Peter, where're your manners? Give the lady a clean glass."

The waiter took Amanda's glass, wiped off the lipstick with his dirty apron, and put it back in front of her."

"Now, that's better," Otto said with a smirk.

"I need to know why Marlene was here the Thursday before she died. It's very important," she said, hoping that she sounded confident and strong.

Otto reached into his vest pocket and took out what looked like a small enameled pen. He pressed a ruby on the side, and five golden wires came out of one end. The center wire was longer than the other four and had a diamond mounted at the tip. Amanda watched as he put this elaborate swizzle stick into his champagne and stirred. The bubbles, which took years to form in the caves of Épernay, foamed to the top, and all effervescence left the wine.

He looked at her for a moment. "Marlene dropped by often," he said. "It was a kind of escape for her."

"In what way?"

"She came here to meet men and gamble in the back room. Your friend was no angel."

"Do you know any of the men she met? Can you describe them?"

"I don't give out that kind of information."

Amanda sank back into her chair.

"I've created a place here—a kind of home away from home where people can come to let their hair down. In spite of what you might think of my little establishment, a lot of your hoity-toity society comes here when they want to let go." He continued to stir the now-lifeless champagne. "They wouldn't come back if I was loose with their names, now would they?"

Before Amanda could respond, a loud drum roll sounded from the stage. An MC in a brocade jacket ran up the few stairs into the spotlight and grabbed the microphone. The white makeup adorning his thin face made his skin appear bleached out, in contrast to his false eyelashes and red lipstick.

"*Meine Damen und meine Herren*, it is now time for our midnight show." At the sound of his falsetto voice, a hush came over the room. "Chez Otto is pleased to present the sexy, the spectacular, the sensational Seglenda!"

A voluptuous redhead slunk onto the stage in a black sequined gown. It had a high neckline and a slit up the skirt revealing long shapely legs. Black satin gloves stretched to her elbows. She took the microphone and shook her shoulders, causing her ample breasts to bounce to the accompaniment of a drum roll. A roar of approval and whistles rose from the crowd.

Amanda looked at Otto. He had turned away from her and was staring transfixed at Seglenda, who began singing in a throaty voice. She rocked her hips to a seductive few bars from the saxophone, raising cheers from the audience.

The bouncer appeared at their table and whispered something into Otto's ear. Otto turned to Amanda, "I'm needed in the back room. Stay as long as you like. Drinks are on the house." He got up and put his hand on her shoulder. "Marlene was looking for trouble. She brought it all on herself. Take my advice and forget about her."

He left in a fog of tobacco smoke. She sat for a while watching the stage show, wondering what to do next. Unwanted attention from men at a nearby table added to her discomfort.

After a medley of sultry songs, Seglenda took bow after bow to thunderous applause. Then, waving to her fans, she exited through a pair of curtains to the left of the stage as the next act entered from the right.

Amanda got up and went after her. If Seglenda did her act every night, she would surely have noticed Marlene and any men she might have been with. Amanda quickly ducked behind the curtains, but the singer had already disappeared.

She found herself in a hallway dimly lit by tarnished metal satyrs holding dusty glass globes. The red flocked wallpaper was peeling in several places beneath a tin ceiling.

A light from under a doorway at the end of the hall drew her attention. She approached and knocked lightly.

After a few seconds and some shuffling sounds, she heard a sexy "Please come in."

Amanda entered the dressing room and found Seglenda stretched out in a dramatic pose on a tattered silk chaise lounge. One hand was behind her head, her hair covered one eye, and her skirt was open to the top of her thigh.

When she saw Amanda, she swung her long legs over the side and sat upright. "I was expecting one of my fans," she said in a distinctly different voice.

"I'm sorry to bother you, but it's important."

Seglenda went behind a screen. "This dress is so tight I can hardly breathe." When the singer came from behind the screen, he had on a blue terry robe, and the long red hair was in his hand. He hung the wig on a peg, sat at a dressing table, and removed his false eyelashes. "Don't look so surprised," he said. "I'm a female impersonator, sort of on my European tour, ya know—Paris, London, Rome, Cologne. When you're hot, you're hot, if you know what I mean. In New York, I'm known as Romping Rita after my Rita Hayworth impressions. Now that woman had a body. I changed my act a little for the European crowd."

Amanda sat on the chaise as Seglenda slapped a glob of cold cream on his face.

"You're American too, right?" he said to her.

"Right. New York."

"It's nice to see a fellow New Yorker. When you get back home, come and see my act in the Village." He smiled as he tissued off the heavy makeup. "It feels good to take this crap off my face. My pores are screaming for oxygen." The hairnet came off, releasing a shiny brown ponytail. "By the way, who are you, and why are you back here? I doubt you're after my autograph."

"I wanted to ask you if you happened to see an attractive blonde woman on a Thursday night two weeks ago, my business partner, Marlene Eichler."

"Honey, I see a lot of people. I can't possibly remember them all."

"It's terribly important."

His features softened as he turned around to face her. "My real name is Harry Phillips, by the way."

"I'm Amanda Lee."

"What does your friend look like?"

She took a picture of Marlene out of her purse and showed it to him.

"Oh yes. Always in haute couture?"

Amanda nodded.

"Hey, you look a lot like her. Sure, you couldn't help but notice her. She had class—attracted men like a magnet."

"Did you see her in here on a Thursday night? It would have been two weeks ago."

Wild applause was audible from out front. The band was playing bump-and-grind music.

"When the strippers are on you can hardly hear yourself think," he said. "Hmmm. It's hard to remember. Every night's the same."

"It would have been the last time she was here," Amanda said.

"Oh, yeah, I remember now. She had some kind of fight with Otto. I was on stage and couldn't hear what was said, but they had words. She seemed very upset. He walked away from her, and she left."

"Can you remember any of the men she might have met here?"

"There was one man who was all over her. She encouraged him at first, but later there was trouble in paradise. I remember one night, they—or rather she—invited me to join them for a drink. She had grown contemptuous of him. He didn't like it one bit. He gave her a look that gave me the willies. He was the controlling type, ya know. I could tell he wanted to slap her around good, but she just ignored him. She as much as told him to get lost."

"What did he look like?" Amanda asked.

"He was tall, good-looking in a kiss-my-ass sort of way."

"What was his name?"

Harry grabbed Amanda's arm as an expression of surprise and pain crossed his face. A trickle of blood rolled down his chin, as he fell into her lap.

"Harry. Harry."

He was unresponsive. She gasped as she saw the bullet hole in the side of his head. The door was partially open, and she heard a scuffle of footsteps move quickly down the hall. She felt for a pulse. Harry was dead.

CHAPTER 15

Amanda's blood thundered in her ears as she tip-toed to the dressing room door and looked out. There was no one in the hallway. To the left were the curtains where she had entered this *Alice in Wonderland* rabbit hole. She could not go out that way. To the right was a red light marked *Ausgang*. Thank God.

The fire exit opened into an alley filled with puddles of icy water. Her suede shoes squished as she ran in what she hoped was the right direction. What if the killer had also come this way? Every shadow seemed to be reaching out for her. At the end of the alley, she was relieved to see her car still parked where she'd left it. Seconds later she was roaring down the unfamiliar streets. *The police!* She had to call the police. Making a wild U-turn, she screeched to a halt in front of a phone both. She rum-maged in her purse for coins and dialed Grutzmacher's number. "Kommissar Grutzmacher went home hours ago," said a weary male voice.

"I must speak to him," Amanda said.

"What is this all about?"

"There's been a murder at Chez Otto. It just happened a few minutes ago. A female impersonator named Seglenda or rather Harry Phillips."

"Please calm down and tell me your name, address, and telephone number."

"Hurry. The killer may still be there."

"First your name, address, and telephone number." The voice was slow, deliberate, and maddening. She rushed through the information requested and told the story again. Her breath was coming in short, shuddery gasps.

"Are you calling from Chez Otto?" the officer asked.

"No, a phone booth. I was afraid I'd be killed too."

"We'll send a car over there. Go home and wait for our call."

Amanda found her way onto the Autobahn. She kept an eye on the rearview mirror. No one was following her.

It felt good to be home. To sooth her nerves, she poured a good stiff brandy and sank into the leather sofa. Regen jumped up onto her lap. His low rhythmic purring and the brandy gradually calmed her down. After a while, she dozed off.

The sound of the telephone seemed to be coming from far away. It must have rung half a dozen times before she fully woke up and remembered what had happened. She picked up the receiver. "Hello."

"Frau Lee? Is this the residence of Frau Amanda Lee?"

"Yes," she said, trying to focus her mind.

"This is Officer Müller. Are you the person who reported the murder at Chez Otto*?*"

*"*Yes."

"Well, Frau Lee, you were, shall we say, mistaken or else trying to play a joke, yes?"

"I don't joke about murder. I was there when it happened."

"We investigated your allegation. When we arrived, Seglenda was performing on stage, very much alive. We searched her dressing room and the entire place and found nothing. No one knew anything about a murder. Are you there, Frau Lee?"

"That's impossible."

"Are you aware it is a criminal offense to turn in a false report?"

℘℘℘

Friday morning, an anemic sun peeked from behind threatening clouds. Dieter Becker strode to his car and used a gloved hand to sweep light frost from the windshield. It was almost seven o'clock, early for him, but on the day he taped his show, *Speaking of Art*, he liked to be there ahead of time to make sure preparations went smoothly.

Today, he was doing a retrospective on the work of Joseph Beuys. He'd borrowed various works from local collectors to give his viewers a glimpse of Beuys's art not seen by the general public. There was a large sculpture that had been difficult to move and reassemble, but it was striking in its magnitude. By contrast, he would also show delicate drawings done in animal blood of the elk, the stag, and the swan. According to Beuys, they represented "figures which pass freely from one level of existence to another." Dieter liked the intellectual tone of that quote. He would use it.

He had been fortunate enough to find rare photographs of Beuys on holiday, wearing his familiar felt hat even at the beach. Beuys had made quick sketches in the sand, barely recorded by the photographer before they were washed away.

Ordinary people are born every second, Dieter thought, *but a relatively small number of great artists such as Beuys ever grace this earth.* There were only a handful alive today. All too many were pretenders, making ridiculous scribbles signifying nothing but a bankruptcy of their creativity. Stopping at a red light near the Kölner Dom, he looked up at the twin Gothic spires. The historic cathedral remained undiminished by wars and the passing of centuries. This was art.

As he drove on, his mind drifted to Amanda. She had

been one of the few to see Kruger's work for what it was—garbage. Secretly, he admired her for that. She hadn't been dazzled by Dieter's own full-throated endorsement. He'd let her squirm long enough. Tomorrow he'd ring her for lunch. There was something important he had to discuss with her.

❦❦❦

"Has Unter Kommissar Rudolf come in yet?" Grutzmacher asked. "Not yet," replied a voice from the intercom. "There was a call for you last night from a Frau Amanda Lee. She reported a murder at Chez Otto, but the responding officers found that no such crime had been committed."

"Bring me that report and a cup of coffee." *My God*, he thought, *what was she doing there?* It was a known underworld hangout and a new favorite of the playful rich. Grutzmacher had heard from informants that Otto himself was involved in contract killings and drug deals, in addition to his legitimate businesses, but there was never any proof. As he sipped his coffee, he read over the police report, then picked up the phone and dialed Amanda's number. "Frau Lee?"

"Yes."

"Fredrich Grutzmacher here. I understand you ran into a bit of trouble at Chez Otto last night. I just read the report."

"To say the least," she said. "I don't know who this other Seglenda is, but it was not the one I talked to. He's dead."

"He?"

"Yes, a female impersonator from New York named Harry Phillips. He died in my arms from a bullet to the head."

"Would you be willing to go back there with me to-night to question this other Seglenda?"

"Then you believe me?"

"I simply want to clear up a few things. The uniformed officers found nothing. You know that."

"I don't care. He was there just as I described."

"I'll pick you up around eleven. By the way, what were you doing at a place like Otto's?"

Amanda hesitated. "Marlene was there the Thursday night before she died. According to Harry, alias Seglenda, she had a fight with Otto. She was also there on several occasions with a mystery man.

"Did he identify the man?"

"No. He died before he could give me a name."

෭෨෭෨

Wolf Eichler walked along Düsseldorf's Königsallee toward his office. It was too early for the shops to be open. He passed by without seeing them and crossed the stone bridge over the small canal that ran through the middle of the street and stopped for a moment to look down at two swans gliding gracefully near its banks. The chilly morning air carried the melodious sound of water rushing from the mouth of an ancient stone Neptune directly beneath him.

He continued on toward the elegant skyscraper that bore his name and housed his offices.

When he was in school, his teachers had informed his mother that his IQ would allow him to become whatever he wanted to be. His father, however, a man of modest means and ambitions, advised him not to get his hopes up. "We are just average people Wolf, as were our fathers before us. Dreaming too big only leads to disappointment."

But Wolf was a dreamer and saw past the "average" to the endless possibilities that awaited him. His mother used to tell his teachers, "Wolf lives in a world of his own making. He was born to his father and me, but speaks in ways that are alien to us."

When he was seven years old, she took him on a free tour of the new Düsseldorfer building. It was a modern phenomenon at the time.

"When I grow up, I want to make buildings like this," he had told her.

"You mean you want to be an *architekt*," she said.

Architekt. He loved the sound of the word, the physical feeling of saying it. He repeated it over and over again, tasting it, savoring it, digesting its meaning.

When his schoolmates were making drawings of cats and dogs, he drew tall buildings strongly rooted in their foundations, with their heads in the sky. Over the years his talent stood out, and his teachers saw to it that he received scholarships to the best schools. Now here he was, at the top of his profession, most of his life goals accomplished.

However, there was something missing that nagged him when he was alone.

He thought of Amanda and was filled with anticipation—the possibility, anyway—of something wonderful happening. It wasn't just about sex. It was much more than that: the way he felt when he was with her—a rare happiness, even in the midst of all that was going on. He wanted to see her. He had to see her. He'd call and invite her to the opera tomorrow night. His pace quickened as he entered the Eichler Building.

ल्ञल्ञ

A sense of melancholy surrounded Amanda as she unlocked the door to the gallery. The place was as dark and gloomy as the weather outside. There was no cheery hello from Rolf, no smell of fresh coffee. And she missed Marlene. Hard to believe the Marlene she had known could be involved with creeps like Demuth and Otto and maybe worse. She must have been driven by the loneliness she had known since she was abandoned as a child.

Amanda flipped on the lights and went into her office. The mail was piling up, and right on top was a bill from Sophia Danielle's boutique. There had to be some mistake. Amanda had paid Sophia for her one shopping spree there. Ripping open the envelope, she saw the bill was for a dress purchased by Marlene for a whopping DM 3,000. She certainly had no intention of paying this without at least a description of the garment so she could make sure it was in Marlene's closet.

Tossing the bill aside, she went through the rest of the mail and found a couple of acceptances for the Reed opening. There was far less interest than there had been for Kruger. But then, Dieter Becker had not reviewed Reed. In fact, Dieter had not spoken to her since she told him about the show.

She picked up the phone and called Rolf. "How are you today?"

"I'm feeling much better. If you can stand looking at a few bruises, I'll try to come in tomorrow."

"Only if you're okay. I must admit I miss you."

As she hung up the phone, she became aware of the delicate scent of Wolf's flowers. It had only been a few days since their dinner date, but it felt like an eternity. The phone rang, and she was not surprised to hear his voice when she answered it. "I was just thinking about you," she said.

"Well, that's a good sign. I wonder if you would like to attend the Düsseldorf opera with me tomorrow night."

"I'd love to."

"I have a late meeting in Cologne. I'll call for you tomorrow at seven."

ೞೞೞ

That evening, Grutzmacher picked her up as promised. At least he was following up on her story. Neither said a word as they barreled toward Chez Otto at Autobahn speeds. *I hope we don't crash*, thought Amanda.

When they reached the after-hours club, the same bouncer as the night before opened the door. He did not look happy to see them.

Grutzmacher flashed his badge. "Where's Otto?"

They were shown to the same dark table at the rear of the club.

Otto indicated a couple of chairs. "Have a seat." To Amanda, he said, "You've got some weird sense of humor."

"Really?" Grutzmacher said.

"Yeah," Otto said. "She came in here last night asking all kinds of questions about her partner and my patrons. When I wouldn't tell her anything, she pulled that stunt of calling the police and saying there was a murder. They questioned customers and harassed my star. That's very bad for business." He clucked his tongue and shook his head at Amanda.

"There was a murder," she said, "and you know it."

Otto expelled a cloud of cigar smoke. "Then where's the body?"

The pasty-faced MC ran up the bandstand steps and announced Seglenda's act. A tall, voluptuous redhead in a skintight black gown burst onto the stage. She took the mic and shook her shoulders causing her ample breasts to bounce in time to a drum roll.

It was a replay of last night. Amanda felt as if she were doing combat duty in the twilight zone. Whoever this was performed exactly the same songs in the same suggestive way. Over the faulty sound system, even her voice sounded identical to Harry's. Could it be Harry? No, she saw him die.

At the end of the performance, Otto led the way to the star's dressing room and knocked. A sexy voice said, "Come in, please."

They entered to find the singer already behind a screen. "You'll have to excuse me, but I have to get out of this dress. It's so tight I can hardly breathe." The same words Harry had used. When she came from behind the screen, she had on a blue robe just like Harry's, but the red hair and bosom were still in place.

"These people seem to think you're dead," Otto said.

"Well, that's not very flattering," she breathed.

"I'm Kommissar Grutzmacher, and this is Frau Amanda Lee. Last night she witnessed the death of a female impersonator named Harry Phillips who used the stage name Seglenda."

"There is only one Seglenda," she said, "and if I'm a female impersonator, I do one hell of a good job." She opened her robe to reveal her large breasts and other feminine attributes.

"We don't have female impersonators here," Otto said. "Frau Lee might have had a bit too much to drink last night. I ordered her a whole bottle of champagne."

"Is that true?" Grutzmacher asked Amanda.

"Yes, but—"

"Mix alcohol with a few drugs and you might start having hallucinations—about murder for instance," Otto said.

Amanda started to object and decided it was useless. The current Seglenda lit a cigarette, blowing the smoke into Amanda's face.

"Frau Lee, I think you'd better come with me," Grutzmacher said as he took Amanda by the arm.

CHAPTER 16

Amanda couldn't wait to get away from Otto's. As if in response to her wish, Grutzmacher's car lurched forward, tires squealing over the cobblestones. "Thanks for your vote of confidence," she said. "It's nice to know you take the word of a sleaze like Otto and his fake Seglenda over mine."

"Perhaps we should go somewhere for coffee and discuss this matter further," Grutzmacher said.

"I just want to go home," she said. "We can talk on the way."

"Very well. How do you account for the fact that your 'victim' is alive and well and performing at Otto's?"

"That was not the same person."

"The Seglenda we just questioned fit your description exactly, except for the part about being a man. Could you be mistaken about that?"

"I certainly know the difference between a man and a woman. This creature we met tonight was an impostor. It's true she was wearing the same dress, probably the same wig. My guess is she's one of the strippers. That would also account for her knowing Harry's act."

Grutzmacher's face flickered first red, then blue, then yellow as they passed beneath neon lights beckoning now to empty streets.

"There was plenty of time to get rid of the body before the police got there. And if they believed Otto, as you apparently do, that the whole thing was a hoax, they may not have bothered to investigate thoroughly."

"I'm not taking anything at face value," he said. "I'll have Rudolf check with Pass Control to see if a work visa was issued to a person known as Harry Phillips."

Amanda began to feel a little better. They would surely be able to substantiate Harry's existence. Leaving the sleeping city, they merged onto the rain-slicked pavement of the Autobahn. The image of Harry's twisted face haunted Amanda's mind.

※

At ten o'clock the next morning, Amanda arrived at the gallery. The wonderful aroma of coffee greeted her at the door. Rolf was back.

She ran into the office. "Rolf, I'm so glad to see you. You have no idea how much I've missed you—and your coffee."

"I've missed you too."

She gave him a hug then looked at his bruised face. His arm was in a sling. "Do you really feel well enough to be here?"

"Absolutely. Lying in bed makes me crazy." He poured them each a cup of coffee. "Dieter Becker called to invite you to lunch today. I told him you'd be there. Twelve-thirty at the Klimt."

❡❡❡

Amanda was the first to arrive. She was shown to a table next to the window. People rushed past with brightly wrapped packages, trying to crowd some early Christmas shopping into the lunch hour.

Two attractive young women stopped near the taxi stand. They were laughing and enjoying themselves, much as she and Marlene had done only a short time ago. How she wished she could close her eyes and open them to find Marlene seated across from her.

"Hello, my dear." Dieter's face was flushed from the cold.

"It's good to see you," Amanda said.

After ordering a white wine and a pilsner, they sat perusing the menu. There was some strained small talk about how she'd been and Dieter's latest TV show. She could tell he was still miffed at her for giving up Kruger and selecting her own artist.

"I'm sorry I didn't tell you about Gregg Reed earlier," she said, deciding to tackle the problem head on, "but I thought it was time I chose the artists for the gallery. It's not that I'm ungrateful for all you've done. Surely you realize that."

"I admit I was more than a little upset. After all, I've gone to great lengths to promote the gallery. That's one of the reasons you've enjoyed so much success."

"I realize that, Dieter. You've been very generous. But it also afforded you a convenient venue to promote your favorite artists." *Many of whom are as creative as this basket of bread*, Amanda thought.

His tone turned to friendly concern, "I'm worried about you. This town can be very fickle when it comes to art and to galleries. My stamp of approval equals success, if I do say so myself."

"You have a great deal of influence, no question."

He nodded at the acknowledgment and took a long drink of his beer. "I would like to continue to be of assistance, my dear. You need me now more than ever. For one thing, you're an outsider here—a very attractive one, but an outsider nevertheless. Without my assurances as to the value of the art you show, many people will not feel comfortable buying it."

"I am also an expert in contemporary art. I handled and collected works by many notable artists in New York."

"Aaah, but this is Germany."

"I've been here almost two years," she said.

"Let me put it to you this way. If I chose to live in America, I would eventually become an American. But a foreigner who lives in Germany can never be considered a German and certainly not a real expert on anything German. Without my support, you will eventually go under."

"Is that a threat?"

"No, that's a fact. I suspect you're already hurting. How many acceptances have you received for this fellow's opening?"

Amanda took a sip of wine but didn't answer.

"I thought so. Marlene was the contact with the public. Before the Kruger opening, no one even knew who you were. I rarely saw you myself until after Marlene's death."

"I was very busy—"

"In the background. Though what you did was the guts of the business, no one knew it but you, Marlene, and me."

"I've been telephoning our clients. They know me now."

"But not well enough. Neither they nor I have ever heard of this what's-his-name. How many of his paintings do you think you'll sell?"

"His name is Gregg Reed." Amanda was starting to lose her appetite.

"Right. Please understand. I am very fond of you."

He downed the last of his beer and signaled for another. "I've rather enjoyed being involved with the gallery."

"Then maybe you could come by and look at Reed's paintings. Once you've seen them, I think you'll agree his work is fresh, optimistic, and original. He's really a contemporary genius. Just read some of these reviews from New York." Amanda took newspaper and magazine clippings from her purse and put them in front of Dieter.

He ignored them. "I will be happy to look at your artist. But first I'd like to make a small proposal."

"What kind of proposal?"

Dieter leaned forward and spoke softly. "I want to help select all of your artists. Confidentially, of course, just as we have in the past. I could even invest a little money, be a kind of silent partner."

"Dieter, I appreciate the offer, but I want to run my own business. Can't we have a normal critic/gallery owner relationship? You review my artists honestly and report your opinions to your readers, as you do with other galleries."

"I'm sorry, my dear, but the Lee Eichler is not like other galleries. I've been involved since day one, and I want to continue to be involved. It's really best for all concerned."

You mean it's best for you, Amanda thought. "Please Dieter, try to understand. I can't take you on as a partner. Isn't that considered conflict of interest or something?"

"How so?"

"It would be like a New York theater critic investing money in a play, then giving it rave reviews. It's dishonest."

"You are so naïve, my little one." His smile had vanished, and his eyes looked at her as if she were a stranger. "You think it over, and get back to me when you've reached the intelligent decision. I can wait. Can you?" Dieter opened his newspaper and began to read his own column, dismissing her.

Amanda knew he'd be annoyed, but she never expected this. "Goodbye, Dieter."

Grabbing her coat from the rack, she walked out into the crowd of holiday shoppers. She felt like she had just been punched in the stomach. This had been his plan all along, the real reason he had helped to get the gallery started. He never intended to get out of the picture. He thought she would be more dependent than ever when Marlene died, and it hadn't worked out that way. Well, he could not force her into a secret partnership.

Pausing for a moment, Amanda gazed into a toy store window. Animated figures danced in slow, jerky movements. A bear, a ballerina, and a clown raised their arms and twirled round and round on their brightly painted pedestals. Well, Amanda would not dance to his tune. Still, she knew Dieter could hurt her simply by doing nothing.

What if she lost the gallery? She'd worked night and day to make it a success. Marlene had too. She couldn't let all they'd struggled for go up in flames, nor would she let Dieter take over.

Rolf was opening the mail when she walked in. "How's the response to the Reed show?"

He held up a couple of RSVPs. "Well, they aren't exactly breaking down the doors. How did it go with Dieter? When is he coming over to review Reed's work?"

"He's not," Amanda said. "We can no longer count on Dieter Becker for anything."

"Then we're doomed," Rolf said. "What happened?"

"We'll discuss it later."

"By the way, Wolf Eichler called and said he'd pick you up at seven."

☙☙☙

Amanda and Wolf sat in the orchestra surrounded by a glittering crowd of Düsseldorf's well-heeled citizens.

"You look beautiful in green velvet," he whispered, putting his hand over hers.

As the lights dimmed and the overture to *La Traviata* began, Amanda felt completely removed from her problems, lost in the richness of Verdi's music and the nearness of Wolf. He held her hand, and she found herself wondering if this was the one she had dreamt of, longed for.

At intermission, they walked out to the champagne bar.

"To us," he said, touching her glass with his and looking at her in a way that made her feel warm and wanted. He leaned down to kiss her.

"Wolf darling, where have you been, you naughty boy? You haven't called in weeks."

Amanda turned to see a striking woman of about thirty-five in a strapless black gown. She moved between Amanda and Wolf, placing a possessive arm around his waist.

"Baroness Petra von Rumohr, this is Amanda Lee."

Amanda held out her hand, but the baroness ignored it, turning back to Wolf. "You've been very bad not calling, wasting time with little distractions, but I've decided to forgive you."

Doubt plagued Amanda once more as she wondered how many baronesses, shop girls, and secretaries had Wolf been with, all of them hoping he would succumb to their charms.

"Be at my party next Friday, at eight o'clock. See you then."

Before he could respond, the baroness kissed him on the mouth and glided off to join her friends.

The excitement and gaiety that had filled the atmosphere only moments before evaporated for Amanda. This woman and Wolf were obviously lovers. Well, what did she expect? He was an attractive and successful man. Of course, women were all over him. She had a strange and uneasy feeling—a twinge of jealousy, perhaps? Moving to the mezzanine banister, she looked down on the crowd. Poinsettias and candlelight decorated the great hall. She could feel Wolf move in close behind her. In such a short while, he had come to mean…well, to be important to her.

"I'm sorry. Petra is a very spoiled and impetuous woman."

"You are certainly entitled to have other friends."

"We had a brief affair. It's over, and she knows it." Gently, he kissed Amanda's neck. "I haven't dated another woman since I met you. Nor do I want to."

❧❧❧

After the opera, they drove out of downtown Düsseldorf, taking the Hofgartenrampe along the Rhine, heading toward Oberkasseler Brücke. The bridge was strung with a necklace of lights, which, in fog, took on the luminosity of pearls.

"Oberkassel is one of the city's few districts left intact by the war," he said.

They passed street after street of expensive homes with wide lawns and tree-lined walkways.

"Is the restaurant far?" she said.

"Not very."

Amanda was surprised when they pulled into the circular drive of an impressive three-story *Jugendstil* house. "How do you like it?" he said.

"Art Nouveau. It's beautiful."

"I hope you don't mind, but I've arranged for a light supper here rather than share you with a crowded restaurant. Anna, my new cook, is fantastic."

Flowing asymmetrical lines were carved into the rich cherry wood of the doorway. The door was embellished with stained-glass panels. They entered a long hallway with a white marble floor. Amanda stood for a moment to take it all in. Wolf gave her a squeeze and took her coat. "August Endell designed it around 1904. I was going to build something contemporary, but I fell in love with this house the moment I saw it."

"I can see why."

At the end of the hall was a curved staircase, also made of cherry. Its balustrades echoed the same free-form organic pattern.

"Hungry?"

"Starved."

As they headed into the dining room, there was the wonderful aroma of roasted pheasant. The table was set with Meissen china, crystal, and antique silverware. White roses and candles made up the centerpiece.

A portly gray-haired woman came out of the kitchen and was introduced as Anna. "You are ready for *abendessen, ja*?" she said.

"We can hardly wait," Wolf said, holding a chair for Amanda. "Thank you for coming in on Saturday and making this fantastic meal."

Anna beamed at the acknowledgement.

For a starter, she served oysters in champagne sauce. They were delicious with the dry white wine Wolf had selected. Next came the pheasant accompanied by crisp, young vegetables and crushed black truffle. Anna cleaned up and left so discreetly, they didn't hear her go.

Wolf opened the French doors to the study where they were greeted by the warmth of the fireplace. An eclectic mix of furniture and paintings gave the room a comfortable elegance. Coffee and brandy had been laid out near the fire.

Wolf took Amanda's hand and kissed the palm. "Since first we met, I've thought of what it would be like to have you here."

Soft piano music drifted in from an unseen stereo.

"Did Marlene ever live in this house?" Amanda said.

"No. I bought it after we separated."

"What happened to your marriage?"

"Marlene needed a great deal of attention. I was busy growing my business and couldn't spend enough time with her. She didn't understand this, and it led to problems."

They sat in silence for a while, looking into the fire. Then Wolf leaned over and kissed Amanda. She wanted to give in to the emotions that were flooding to the surface, but she wasn't sure. What if he considered her just another affair, like that baroness? What if he turned out to be another Karl? She really didn't know him all that well.

She pulled away. "The dinner was lovely, Wolf. I enjoyed it very much. Now I'd better be going. I have a show coming up and a lot of to do."

"Amanda, please don't go."

What should she do? She wanted to stay, but she knew she should leave, now. "I have to." She avoided looking into his eyes.

"You've changed my life, whether you meant to or not," he said. "I don't want you to go, ever."

Gently pulling away, she went into the hallway. They put on their coats and headed outside. A light snow blanketed the streets, and the full moon looked close enough to touch. "It will take a few minutes to warm up the car," he said.

"Wait," Amanda said, not caring about all the rationalizations she had made for herself. She put her arms around him and kissed him, hesitantly at first, then passionately. He pulled her back inside. They climbed the beautiful curved staircase shedding their coats along the way.

In the dim bedroom, he carefully removed her green velvet dress. Gently he released the catch of her black lace bra. He stood for a moment looking at her as if he couldn't believe she was really there. Then he began to kiss her lips, her neck, her breasts.

Moments later, they were on the feathery softness of eiderdown. A golden pool of moonlight shining through a frosty window gave everything a surreal halo. She could feel the supple movement of his back, his muscular loins.

Afterward, he held her so close she could hear his heart beating. Snuggling into the curve of his arm, she allowed herself to feel a quiet happiness. For a while she watched shadows dance on the ceiling, and then sank into a peaceful sleep.

બબબ

A rapid pounding on the front door jarred her awake. Wolf slipped on a robe and went downstairs. According to her watch, it was only six a.m.

"Police!" a voice boomed from below. Wrapping herself in a sheet, she tiptoed to the bedroom door and listened.

"Herr Eichler, do you have a housekeeper named Markrit Algar?"

"Yes."

"She's been murdered. Please get dressed and come with us."

CHAPTER 17

I can't imagine who would want to harm Markrit," Wolf said, throwing on his clothes. "I shouldn't be long, Amanda. They've asked me to identify the body. She has no relatives or close friends in Düsseldorf. When I return, I'll take you home," he said, kissing her softly.

❧❧❧

The morgue was damp and cold. The sickeningly sweet smell of death hung in the air. Wolf followed Unter Kommissar Jost of the Düsseldorf police and the medical examiner along a short passageway. Their footsteps on the painted concrete echoed off the walls. The overhead fluorescents distorted reality into sharp contrasts of light and dark.

The three men entered a large gray room in the center of the lower level. The walls were lined with stainless steel doors about a meter square. There were black numbers on each door.

At number 113 they stopped. The medical examiner, a small balding man with a drooping mustache, released the door latch and rolled out a slab on which lay a petite body under a white covering. He took a corner of the fabric and pulled it back. Her skin, pale olive in life, was ashen with a bluish-green tinge.

"Do you know this woman?"

"Yes. Her name is Markrit Algar. She was a guest worker from Turkey," Wolf said, grabbing his handkerchief to cover his nose. As he looked down at his former housekeeper, he had to fight to keep from throwing up. Mercifully, the ME covered the body and pushed the slab back into the vault, slamming the door.

"Does she have any relatives in Germany?"

"She has one son who lives in Munich. It was my impression that she was going to visit him during her holiday."

"Do you know who would want to kill her?"

"No."

"We have a few more questions for you, sir," Jost said. "Would you mind coming down to headquarters?"

With his long sharp nose and closely set eyes, the man reminded Wolf of a rodent.

"I will help in any way I can."

At police headquarters, Wolf was surprised to en-counter Ernst Rudolf.

"We are cooperating with the Cologne authorities in this matter," Jost said.

Wolf looked at Rudolf. "But why? What has this got to do with you?"

"A coincidence perhaps, first your ex-wife, now your housekeeper. Do you own a nine-millimeter handgun, Herr Eichler?" Rudolf strode around the small window-less room with his hands behind his back.

"No," Wolf said.

"But you do own the set to which this belongs." Ru-dolf held up a plastic evidence bag containing a familiar blue and gold tuxedo shirt stud. "This was found in the dead woman's apartment."

"Good Lord. Do you really believe I go about mur-dering people then leave antique studs behind like bread-crumbs to lead you directly to me? That's preposterous. Where is Kommissar Barth? I want to see him. Now!" Wolf shouted at Jost.

"I am sorry, Herr Eichler, he's not here at the mo-ment." Jost fidgeted with his pen, avoiding Wolf's eyes.

"We are only interested in clearing this up." Rudolf's voice had taken on a conciliatory tone.

"Someone is obviously trying to frame me. That should be clear enough. When was Markrit killed?"

"The coroner's best guess is last Thursday," Jost said. "The body wasn't discovered until late last night.

When she didn't arrive in Munich, her son became worried. After repeatedly trying to telephone her, he called the couple living next door to her. They did nothing at first, believing there was some logical explanation—she'd gone shopping or had missed the train. After her son contacted them several times into the next day, they called us."

"And because she was a foreigner, you didn't put her high on your priority list," Wolf said.

"Why didn't you report her missing?" Rudolf's eyes narrowed as he asked the question.

"She went on vacation the day she was murdered and was not due back for over a week."

"And where were you last Thursday night?"

"I was working late at my office."

"Can anyone corroborate that?"

"I was there alone." Wolf looked straight at Rudolf. "If you are going to arrest me, do so. If not, I'm leaving, and any further contact can be through my advocate."

"You are free to go anytime. Thank you for your cooperation."

Wolf saw Rudolf and Jost exchange conspiratorial looks.

ဢ

Wolf's hands were shaking as he put the key into the ignition. When he pulled up in front of his house, it was seven-thirty. The aromas of bacon and coffee greeted him as he entered the house. He headed straight for the kitchen.

"How did it go?" Amanda said.

His silk paisley bathrobe was tied around her slender body. He took her in his arms and held her very close. "They seem to think I had something to do with Markrit's death."

In the car heading toward Cologne, Amanda listened in disbelief as Wolf told her about his discussion with Rudolf.

"He can't really believe it's you," she said. Anxiety and fear for Wolf slowly seeped into her being.

"I guess they are getting desperate. There have now been two murders. First Marlene, now Markrit."

And Harry Phillips, thought Amanda. She hadn't told Wolf about him.

They rode in silence the rest of the way. Wolf dropped Amanda off at her condo, giving her a lingering kiss in the doorway, then took off across the courtyard. She watched till he disappeared, trying to hang on to the comforting warmth she'd felt in his arms.

෴

"How many have accepted for the Reed opening?" Amanda asked.

"About half a dozen." Rolf's face took on a serious

look that seemed at odds with his boyish features. "Without Dieter Becker's recommendation, we're not going to have much of a show."

"Dieter is powerful, but he's not God."

"He is as far as the Cologne art scene is concerned."

Amanda had to think of something. With a little over a week left before the opening, it was too late to start trying to pull people in by phone. Besides, that would give the appearance of desperation. She would not beg Dieter to help her, nor would she give him part of her business. What could she do?

If she didn't pull this off for Reed, artists, as well as collectors, would trivialize her. All of Dieter's ugly predictions would come true. She went into her office and closed the door. Now, with the threat of losing it, she realized more than ever how much this place meant to her. She had to think. Her mother used to say, "There's always a right solution to every problem, no matter how difficult. Just be still and listen. The answer will come from within. The answer will come."

She sat down at her desk and closed her eyes, shutting out the voices of doubt and defeat. After what seemed a long time, the germ of an idea began to stir. She got up and called to Rolf. "Isn't there an American jazz club in the Altstadt?"

"Yes," he said with a curious look. "It's great. They book only the best jazz musicians from the States. That place is always jammed."

"Check and see who's playing there now."

"I already know. It's the Billy Johnson Trio—piano, base, and drums. I have all their CDs."

"Call and see if we can book them for next Wednesday night."

"The night of Reed's show?" Rolf asked.

She nodded.

After a series of calls, Rolf finally got Billy Johnson on the phone. "We can get them," he said after hanging up, "but it's going to cost you. They can only play from six to eight-thirty. The first set at the jazz club is at ten o'clock."

"Book them," Amanda said.

"It's none of my business, boss, but should you be spending big money when we may not make enough to pay our overhead?"

"Please, Rolf, book them." She sat down at her computer, thought for a moment, then wrote, *New York's Hottest Contemporary Artist is now in Cologne.* Then, continuing, *The Lee Eichler Gallery invites you to be among the first to view the works of acclaimed New York artist Gregg Reed from 6:00 p.m. to 8:30 p.m. Wednesday.*

See why the New York critics are raving over Reed, while you listen to the Billy Johnson Jazz Trio. Favorite foods and wines from the United States will be served.

She signed off with, *Lee Eichler, the Gallery of Contemporary American Art.*

Printing out the ad, she handed it to Rolf, telling him

to add in the best quotes on hand from New York critics. "Take a full page in *Der Kölner Zeitung* and run this in tomorrow's edition and every day till the show. Tell them that, from now on, we'll be advertising our openings in their newspaper exclusively. In return, we want positioning opposite Dieter's column. That way, when people interested in art turn to read what's new according to Dieter, they'll see our ad."

"He'll never stand for it," Rolf said.

"The advertising sales department is completely separate from editorial. If we get a written contract and give them our check, it will be a done deal before he finds out."

"Okay," Rolf said.

"From now on, we specialize in American artists. This gives us credibility without Herr Becker and sets us apart from the other galleries. If Dieter doesn't want to give us favorable reviews, we'll quote the critics from the States in thirty-six-point type. They carry more weight than even he does when it comes to American works."

"Amanda, you're brilliant."

"Next, we have to get our hands on some California wine, Virginia ham, and Wisconsin cheese for the party."

Rolf smiled. "My dad has a friend who imports gourmet food. He might be able to help and get us a good price as well. There is one big problem, however."

"What's that?"

"Where are you going to get a piano for Billy Johnson?"

ᚔᚔᚔ

Helga Demuth had barely been out of her bed since
she'd read the report from the private investigator. Lothar
had actually seen Hans kissing that American woman
through the back window of the gallery and snapped a
photo. Nothing had changed. For days, she had wrestled
with the thought of life without Hans. Finally, she'd decided life was much worse as the laughing stock of her
friends. She'd known all along the only thing he truly
cared about was her money.

Eyes swimming with tears, she looked at the bedside
clock. It was two in the afternoon. He had been sleeping
in the guest room since the day she'd confronted him
about Frau Lee. There had been a terrible fight, with
Hans, as usual, denying everything. He'd sounded almost
convincing, but she had the picture to prove her accusa-
tion. Helga wanted nothing more to do with her dear husband.

She heaved her large legs over the side of the feather
bed, stuffed her feet into mink slippers, and padded over
to the closet. Way in the back, she felt for a small box
and pulled it out. A few more large tears traveled down
the bumpy road of her face as she opened it. His bloody
shirt was still there. She printed a note by hand that stated

Hans Demuth had killed Marlene Eichler, and here was the evidence. The label of his tailor appeared at the neck along with the initials H.D. It would be easy to verify the shirt belonged to him. She rang for the maid.

"Wrap this and send it special post to Kommissar Grutzmacher of the police, no return address," she said. "Then book me into the Clinique La Prairie Spa at Clarens-Montreux, Switzerland. When I return, you won't recognize me. It's time for a new husband."

CHAPTER 18

Amanda opened *Der Kölner Zietung* and turned to the arts section. There was her ad, a full page opposite Dieter's column. It looked impressive and should get results even though the tonier galleries here preferred to send their clients private invitations.

She skimmed Dieter's high-flown prose. *There is only one show in the coming week worth seeing, and that's at the Kleinau Gallery. An outstanding collection of contemporary art will be offered...*

Amanda quickly moved through reviews of the various shows until she got to the bottom of the column. *I understand on Wednesday, Gregg Reed, an unknown from America, is showing at Lee Eichler. I wouldn't bother if I were you.*

The raves quoted by the New York art critics in her ad made Dieter's "review" of Reed seem uninformed and unprofessional. She indulged in a little self-congrat-ulation, which was interrupted by the telephone.

Dieter's voice had the sharp edge of a knife. "When you placed this ad, you signed the death warrant for the Lee Eichler Gallery."

A loud click severed the connection before she could say anything.

Amanda sat frozen for a moment, looking at the phone. Never had she heard Dieter's voice filled with such malice. He'd been controlling on occasion but al-ways in a calm, cool way in the guise of helpful advice. There was no doubt about it—he was angry enough to try and ruin her.

Had he approached Marlene with his silent partner proposal, and she'd also said no? Did they have a fight that set him off? Still, it was hard to believe he'd harm her. He'd helped Marlene, loved her in his own way. With her gone, he thought he could just move in and take over. Boy, did he get a wrong number.

She got out Marlene's diary and looked up the entry at noon the Friday before the murder. She'd made a lunch date at Gemütlich Bier Halle with…was that a *D*? Dieter had said he was out of town then, but he could've lied.

D also stood for Demuth. It was time to go down to the Altstadt and check out this restaurant. Maybe a waiter or the owner would remember Marlene and her lunch companion. Amanda hoped for better luck than she'd had at Chez Otto.

The phone again disrupted her thoughts. It was Herr Wiener, the newspaper's advertising manager. "Frau Lee, I regret to inform you we must drop your advertising campaign as of now. A reimbursement check has already been sent by post."

"You signed a contract agreeing to run my ads every day for the coming week. I'll sue you if you don't keep your part of the agreement. My ad had better be in tomorrow's paper."

"That is not possible. I am sorry."

"We'll see," Amanda said and banged down the receiver. A moment later she called Herr Betz. "Can they do this? They only ran the one ad, but I have a contract for four to be run prior to my next opening."

"I'll look into it. Fax me the contract."

At ten that morning, the phone rang again. "I saw your notice in *Der Zeitung,*" said a pleasant female voice. "Do I need to give you my name, or may I just come to the opening?"

"We'd like your name for future invitations."

That was the first call of endless calls that continued throughout the week. Rolf and Amanda answered questions about Reed, his paintings, and the opening in a happy frenzy as they compiled a sizable new mailing list. "This show will be a huge success, no matter what Dieter or his paper does now," Amanda said.

෴

The unter kommissar fairly gloated as he tossed a large envelope onto Grutzmacher's desk. It contained a written report with photos. Making a motion for Rudolf to sit down, Grutzmacher glanced at the top of the document, marked *Volkspolizei–Düsseldorf*, then quickly scanned each point of information.

Name of the deceased: Markrit Algar. Nationality: Turkish. Age: 48. Address: Münster Platz Number 45, Düsseldorf. Employer: Wolf Eichler. Particulars: Female shot 3 times...

Grutzmacher read the remaining information and studied the all-too-graphic photos of another fragile life savagely ended. He read through the list of items found in the victim's handbag. One thing was not mentioned. Keys. Everyone had house keys. After he finished the report, he looked at Rudolf. The man's chin was raised even higher than usual, a self-satisfied smirk on his lips, the arrogant bastard. "How did you find out about this?" Grutzmacher asked.

"If you'll recall, I've always suspected Eichler, perhaps in collaboration with that American woman. I have a friend on the Düsseldorf police force, and I requested he contact me if Eichler so much as got a parking ticket." Rudolf folded his arms across his chest and stretched out his long legs. "It paid off. I was there when they brought him in for questioning."

"Questioning?"

"Yes. To find out where he was at the time of his housekeeper's murder."

"Why would Eichler kill his housekeeper?"

"I think that is obvious. He killed his wife, and the housekeeper saw something that tipped her off. He was afraid she would talk."

"Marlene Eichler was killed with a knife. This woman, Markrit Algar, was shot to death."

Rudolf got up and began pacing the room, gesturing broadly with his hands. "Eichler hated his ex-wife and wanted to make her suffer—to take a long time to die. It was a revenge killing. The housekeeper was just in the way. A gun was the best way to dispatch her."

"And what did he say when questioned about this?"

"Of course, he denied knowing anything about it. Once again no solid alibi. Said he was working at his office alone."

"Maybe he was."

"We found this at the scene." Rudolf pulled an evidence bag from his pocket containing another blue lapis stud.

"It really makes no sense for him to leave that behind—twice," Grutzmacher said. "He's not an idiot."

"Many murderers leave a 'calling card' for some warped reason. He could always say they were stolen from his home, which is exactly what he did say, even though he has a security system that's wired right into police headquarters. It never gave an alarm."

"Was there any other evidence? Fingerprints for example?"

"He must have worn gloves, same as he did with his wife. But this time, we have a witness. As you read in the report, a neighbor saw a strange blond man near the victim's apartment the afternoon she was murdered."

"The report also said the neighbor didn't get a good look at his face," Grutzmacher said, tossing the report to one side. "There are lots of blond men in Germany. For that matter, you're blond. That's no proof. What about a murder weapon?"

"They're still looking for it. They dug nine-millimeter hollow points out of the victim. My friend, Jost, was trying to get a warrant to search Eichler's house for the gun, but a Düsseldorf kommissar is blocking it until all forensic reports are in. Class and money have their privileges. Once again, there was no forced entry. The housekeeper knew her killer and let him in. It was Eichler, no doubt about it."

"What you have so far are circumstantial tidbits mixed with pure conjecture," Grutzmacher said. "Must I remind you that you're not still with the East German Stasi? We do things a bit differently here. We require proof before calling anyone a murderer. The kind that stands up in court."

"Maybe if the law here was enforced a little more like it is in the GDR," Rudolf said, "the crime rate would be considerably less."

εୁ∕ꝫ୯∕ꝫ

A clearly nervous Herr Wiener, the advertising manager of *Der Kölner Zeitung,* stood outside Dieter's office.

"Come in," Dieter said, "come in." Just looking at the man made him furious all over again. "Well? Did you tell her?"

"Yes. I called Frau Lee and told her the ads were canceled, and we were returning her payment."

"Then that's that."

"Not quite." Herr Wiener played with the change in the pocket of his beige cardigan, his weak chin quivering ever so slightly. "She—she is planning to sue the paper. She has a signed contract, Herr Becker. I could lose my job if the managing director finds out about this."

"You could lose your job if you run another one of those ads. I happen to know a great deal about you and some of your little indiscretions. Taking money under the table for better ad placement for example."

Wiener's watery eyes opened wide. "I tried. I was unable to intimidate Frau Lee. You told me that because she was a woman and a foreigner, she would just accept whatever I said. You were wrong." Wiener bit the end of his fleshy lower lip. "What if her lawyer calls the managing director? What then?"

"Then you will be in serious trouble," Dieter said. "Now get out of my sight." After Wiener left, Dieter picked up the phone. "Betts, Becker here. I need a favor."

ℰℴℰℴ

Amanda and Wolf held hands and turned their faces toward the rare and welcome winter sun. They strolled along Düsseldorf's busy Königsalle glancing into richly decorated shop windows on their way to brunch. "I'm so glad it's Saturday," Amanda said. "It's been a pretty rough week."

"Except for one notable occasion," Wolf said, brushing her temple with his lips. "Are you all set for your opening next Wednesday?"

"Yes. No thanks to Herr Becker."

"And what is Dieter up to?"

Amanda told him about her problems and how she had attempted to solve them.

"An ad opposite his column?" Wolf laughed. "What a great idea."

"Well, the one ad worked. The phone hasn't stopped ringing. But the paper is refusing to run follow-up ads. I've asked my lawyer to look into it."

"If you have further problems with Becker or anyone else, I want you to tell me. I'm not without influence, you know."

"It's just that I prefer to deal with these things myself."

"Sometimes, even you may need a little help," he said, giving her hand a squeeze.

They made their way to the Café Goethe, a cozy restaurant at the end of the street. Golden sunlight streamed into the place through arched windows. The aroma of bread fresh from a brick oven mingled with that of rich coffee.

Once they were seated and had ordered, Wolf kissed Amanda's hand. "Are you as happy as I am at this moment?" His eyes held a youthful ardor that belied his sophistication.

"Yes," she said. "When I'm with you, I'm very happy." *But it's not possible to be truly happy*, she thought, *to have a real relationship with you, until Marlene's killer is found.* Whoever he was, he had taken away a friend and left her in a poisonous cloud that permeated everything in her life.

After a leisurely meal, they wandered to a nearby museum. As they entered the Rhinelander Kunsthalle, Amanda was drawn to the portrait of a young woman prominently displayed in the Grand Hall. She sat in profile on a dark-red velvet chair. Her figure was alluring in a creamy silk dress adorned only by a long strand of pearls. Her smooth auburn hair was cut in a flapper bob. It looked French, painted in the early 1930s.

"That is a portrait of Frau Harden," Wolf said, "painted when she was eighteen. It's by Jean-Louis Lorrain, a popular portrait artist of the period. Frau Harden was Dieter Becker's mother."

"Really?" Amanda said. "Her last name is different from his."

"She remarried after his father died. Dieter had plans to become a great artist, but she constantly criticized him. Her rejection of her son caused him to have some kind of breakdown. On his sixteenth birthday, she called the Düssldorf Psychiatrisch Anstalt and had him committed. When they came to get him, he became so violent he had to be taken away in restraints."

"I had no idea."

"I am sure very few people know about it. The family hushed it up. A short time later, Dieter escaped, and before they could catch him, Frau Harden had died from a fatal fall down the stairs. His stepfather accused Dieter of deliberately pushing her. He was sent back to the mental institution under heavy security and remained there for several years."

If this was true, Dieter was capable of murdering someone as close to him as his own mother. Why not Marlene?

"Frau Harden left everything to this museum on the stipulation they always display her portrait in that exact place, overlooking the Grand Hall."

"She left nothing to Dieter?"

"Not a penny. Before his death, Dieter's real father had stipulated that his son would inherit the old family home. If not for that, Dieter would have gotten nothing."

"How do you know all this?"

"My architectural firm did the renovations on this building. I wanted to put a window where the portrait is now, to help increase the light for viewing in this hall, but the curator said no, it could not be moved. I wanted to know why, and he told me the whole story. He is an old man and knew Frau Harden personally."

ை஖ை஖

Amanda and Wolf shared a delicious dinner at his home, prepared once more by Anna. "She has agreed to be both housekeeper and cook," Wolf said.

After dinner, they sipped champagne in the bedroom. Amanda loved this room, the elegant yet masculine feeling so reflective of Wolf, the soft crackling sounds coming from the fireplace, the romantic glow of the candles on the mantel. She ran her fingers over the soft tan suede of the bed cover then curled up in the large, matching wing chair.

Wolf knelt beside her. "I've never known anyone like you," he said softly, kissing the palm of her hand.

He looked up at her—his eyes caressed her, adored her. For Amanda, all of the feelings, all of the searching, all of the longing, seemed to come together in that moment. He did care for her deeply. She could tell. She let this realization wash over her in gentle waves of joy.

"I have a surprise for you," he said.

Amanda put down her glass and followed him. He'd asked Anna to draw a luxurious bubble bath and sprinkle it with fragrant pink rose petals. He removed her clothes as if unwrapping a precious gift. There was no awkwardness between them. He took her hand and helped her into the deep marble bathtub. Amanda closed her eyes as she slipped into the silky, rose-scented water.

✈✈✈

When Sunday morning arrived, snow clouds obliterated the sun. Wolf had to go to Amsterdam on an early afternoon flight. He had dinner plans with his client for Sunday night and a presentation to the museum board of directors on Monday. Looking out of the car window as they sped toward Cologne, Amanda realized she didn't want to go home. She didn't want to be alone. She put her hand on Wolf's arm. He was preoccupied and tense, shutting her out as he retreated into his own private world. It was as if the previous evening had never happened. He barely said a word even when he dropped her off at the condo. Perhaps he was worried about the allegations by the police.

The rest of Sunday stretched before her like a long empty road. The promise of snow became a reality, so she stayed at home with little Regen. The small black cat tried to catch the white flakes that drifted like feathers, touching the French doors before melting. Ice and snow had transformed the trees and bushes of the private garden into glistening sculptures.

She took a book at random from the bookcase, a

slender volume of romantic verse written a century ago by some obscure poet. The title page had an inscription, *To my darling Marlene, with all my love, Wolf.*

The book fell open to page fifteen, and she read:

> *Putting summer things away,*
> *I came across a memory of you.*
> *Though sunny days have turned to gray,*
> *I still recall your eyes of summer blue.*

She stopped reading and closed her eyes for a moment, remembering that Marlene and Wolf had met in summer at *documenta* 6. Gently running her fingers over what appeared to be tiny splashes staining the page, she realized they were from Marlene's tears.

CHAPTER 19

The only thing we can do is to take the newspaper to court. I'm afraid that will cost time and money. I'd advise you against further action in this case…"

"Never mind," Amanda said, banging down the phone.

Dieter had gotten to Betz. Well, it wouldn't affect this show, and that was the main concern at the moment.

The rest of the day was spent making last minute preparations for Wednesday. Reed himself had arrived in Cologne and was staying at the posh Park Hotel across from the dom.

That night, Amanda took him to dinner and went over what she'd planned for the opening. It was good to talk to someone from home. There was an ease of communication she hadn't realized she'd missed. As Marlene once said, "Americans are the masters of nonchalance."

"So, all in all, it looks like it will be quite an event," Amanda said.

"Fantastic," Reed said. "Sounds like you've thought of everything and then some." He was the all-American boy with dark wavy hair.

Amanda couldn't help but think of Superman whenever she looked at him.

The big night arrived, and butterflies danced in her stomach. Looking in the office mirror, she did a final check. The soft winter-white pantsuit was a good choice. It enhanced her blonde hair, which fell smooth and loose, brushing her shoulders. Except for the unicorn bracelet, her only jewelry was a pearl and diamond ring. Marlene would have approved.

Glancing at her watch for the twentieth time, she decided to go through the gallery again. It was five o'clock. The opening was scheduled for six, a full hour earlier than usual to attract people heading home from work. A long table of American food and wine awaited the onslaught of guests. Red, white, and blue flowers formed the centerpiece. The card read, *Good luck tonight, darling. Love, Wolf.*

Four young waiters in American designer jeans and T-shirts printed with one of Reed's paintings busied themselves with plates and glasses.

At five-thirty, the Billy Johnson Trio arrived and set up their equipment around the rented piano. They talked softly as Billy's talented fingers moved over the keyboard, warming up with his improvisation of "Fascinatin' Rhythm." Each canvas was spotlighted in what otherwise resembled a nightclub atmosphere. The paintings displayed energy and an upbeat feeling that seemed to echo the jazz.

"A lot of people will be here tonight for the free food and music," Rolf said. "Many may not have money to buy art."

"Perhaps," Amanda said. "But if enough people see this work and are excited by it, the big collectors will become interested."

A crowd gathered long before six o'clock. When she opened the door, a group of enthusiastic people swarmed in, and the party began. At six-thirty, Gregg Reed arrived. He wore snug-fitting jeans and a red cashmere sweater that showed off his biceps. As Amanda had expected, he was immediately mobbed by young women and some not so young. At seven, Wolf came in with a contingent from Düsseldorf and introduced her to several wealthy collectors. "Thank you," she whispered in Wolf's ear.

He smiled and kissed her. "What are friends for?"

Soon, Rolf was placing red dots next to some of the paintings. Young people who probably had never purchased art before were buying the smaller pieces. Amanda had decided to let them pay in several installments, to encourage them to buy this artist and to build future collections. Some of her old clients began to filter in. Everything was going well. A real charmer, Reed was appealing to the stuffy and wealthy, as well as to the young and cool. Right now, he was engaged in animated conversation with an eighty-year-old baroness.

At seven-thirty, a video crew showed up from Deutsche TV's *What's News in Art*, a competitor of Dieter's channel seen all over Germany. "If you don't mind, we would like to tape some of this for our viewers. It will be on tomorrow afternoon and repeat at six o'clock."

"I don't mind at all," Amanda said.

She was interviewed on the importance of American contemporary art. They took close-ups and long shots of her, the paintings, the crowd, the jazz trio, and of course Reed, who proved to be well spoken and amusing during his interview.

"Dieter will go crazy when he finds out about this," Wolf said, putting his arm around her waist. "You realize, of course, that this television show will be seen prior to his, upstaging any comments he may have about Reed or you."

"Yes. I can't believe how quickly Dieter changed," she said. "One day he was a friend and advisor, the next my archenemy. He was so kind to me after Marlene's death. Now I think he absolutely hates me."

"It's easy to be pleasant when you're getting your way."

The gallery floor was now jammed. Some guests were dancing to Johnson's music. All of them seemed to be having a good time. Amanda checked on the wine and food supply and then led Wolf toward the stairs. "Let's take a look from the catwalk. We can see the whole party from there."

They leaned over the banister and looked down on the crowd.

"You really pulled it off," he said. "I am very proud of you."

It was nice to have someone with whom to share her victory. She felt strong and happy. "Moonlight in Vermont" floated up from below.

He took her into his arms. "May I have this dance?"

As he held her in the shadows of the catwalk, she closed her eyes and drifted into another universe, lost in the exquisite pleasure of his nearness. She wanted this moment to last forever.

"I wish I could stay with you tonight," he said, "But I have another early meeting in Amsterdam."

They continued to hold each other, barely moving as Johnson's trio moved into "Stairway to the Stars."

When the music ended, he leaned down and kissed her—a sweet, lingering kiss—before they reluctantly separated. "I'll call you in the morning." He gently cupped her face with his hands and kissed her once more before heading down the stairs.

If only he could stay. When she was with him, she felt everything would be okay. Funny, Marlene had said the same thing the night before she died.

Amanda remained on the catwalk, watching Wolf make his way through the crowd, stopping here and there to speak to friends. He turned and waved goodbye before disappearing through the door.

꿍

It was a little after nine when Amanda and Rolf locked up. Tired but triumphant, they went out into the freezing night. It began to snow. "We did great," Rolf said. "After the TV show tomorrow, I doubt if we have a single Reed painting left." He lowered his voice. "This is supposed to be a secret, but Wolf Eichler bought a huge painting for his office while you were being interviewed. Many of his friends were also buying. I'd say that we're out of the woods financially, boss."

Amanda started the Porsche. "You were terrific tonight," she told him. "It could never have gone so well without you." She followed his instructions to a modest rooming house on the outskirts of town.

"Goodnight, boss," he said and gave a thumbs up.

He was so loyal, and she was lucky to have him. If there was enough profit after paying the bills, she'd give him a bonus—hopefully enough to replace his motorcycle.

Amanda switched on the radio as she entered the Autobahn. The snow was heavy now. There was no traffic except for one pair of headlights appearing as tiny frosty spots in her rearview mirror. She listened to a local announcer give the end of the news and weather report. "A winter storm advisory is in full effect. Visibility is expected to be near zero with freezing temperatures."

As she made her way along the dark expressway, the car behind her appeared much closer. At least there was someone else on the road if she needed help. That comforting thought shifted quickly into angst as the headlights loomed behind her. They looked like the eyes of a giant cat about to pounce. *He's way too close,* she thought. *He could—*

A crunch of metal rang in her ears as she felt a tremendous jolt. Her head snapped back then forward, hitting the steering wheel. For a moment, she was stunned, spinning round and round in a blur of sleet, snow, and headlights. She grasped the wheel hard as the Porsche skated wildly across the icy pavement. Fighting frantically for control, she steered into the direction of the skid.

When the car came to a halt, she was about ninety meters down the road pointed back toward Cologne. Looking in the rearview mirror, she could only make out brake lights. *That was no accident,* she thought. *God, he's turning around and coming back to finish the job.* Amanda felt too dizzy to drive. She doused the headlights and inched the car off the road.

Frozen grass and small bushes snapped as they were struck by the tires. She drove a short distance and turned off the engine. The wind moaned, and the sleet pecked away at the windshield like a flock of violent birds.

Amanda waited for five, then ten minutes. Had he turned around? Twenty minutes dragged by, and the temperature in the car dropped. She trembled—more from fear than from cold. Her dizziness subsided. Nevertheless, she'd sit tight a little longer to be sure he'd gone. *Who is this man? Could it be Dieter? It's hard to believe he'd do something this reckless, no matter how enraged he became. Then again, he hadn't come up with a single idea concerning Marlene's death painting. Does he know who the artist is? Could he have commissioned the work? Dieter pushed hard for Lee Eichler to show Kruger, a third-rate artist. Could they be in cahoots somehow?*

Thirty minutes, then forty, dragged by. As she reached to start the engine, she saw headlights coming from the direction of Cologne. The windows were fogged from her breath. Using her glove, she wiped away a small patch so she could see. It could be him searching for her or just some tired motorist finding his way home. Better not take a chance. She sat in the icy steel enclosure for another thirty minutes. Her feet were numb. Amanda started the car and felt a frigid blast from the heater. After waiting a few minutes more, she cautiously steered back onto the road and headed home.

꧁꧂

The next morning, Wolf called from Amsterdam and

was furious when she told him about the incident. "If I find out who did this, I'll see that he's put away for a nice long time. Have you made a report to the police?"

"No," she said. "I couldn't see his face or even get a plate number, so I don't know what they can do."

"Call the police and have a phone installed in your car. In the meantime, here's the number where I can be reached."

She wrote it down. "I miss you," she said.

"Take care, Amanda. See you when I return."

She put on her coat, took a Polaroid camera from the hall closet, and headed out to the car. The morning sun was a welcome sight after the storm, but temperatures still felt like the North Pole.

For the first time, she was able to see the damage done to the Porsche. The rear bumper and engine cover had been bashed in, the beautiful lines ruined, and the lipstick-red paint scarred. It brought tears to her eyes to see Marlene's pride and joy in such condition.

But it could have been much worse. At least she hadn't been hurt except for a bump on her forehead and sore neck. She snapped pictures of the damaged back and sides of the car.

The Autobahn had already been cleared and salted, and traffic was moving normally, German efficiency at work. When she reached Cologne, she drove to a repair shop. "This will take a while," the mechanic said, assessing the damage. "Custom paint like this will have to be sent from the factory. And then there are the replacement parts—"

"I also want a car phone installed. When will it be ready?"

"At least a week," the mechanic said. "Maybe more."

"In that case, I'd like a loaner."

He pointed to a black sedan. "The keys are in it."

❧❧❧

Dieter Becker sat in the television studio trying to rewrite his script. Everyone was talking about his feud with the Lee Eichler Gallery. He'd even heard them laughing behind his back. Then there was the problem with Kruger, which was once more getting out of hand. That was the next thing on his agenda.

"Herr Becker, let's go. We have a whole crew waiting for you to begin taping." The director tossed a Coke can into an empty metal waste bin. The nerve-rattling noise advertised his frustration.

"You'll just have to wait till I'm good and ready, old boy. It's my show. I call the shots, and don't you forget it!"

If only he could see a preview of *What's News in Art*. His rival at Deutsche TV would never let that happen, so there was no way he could wangle even a sneak peek. All he could find out was that Amanda had come off as knowledgeable and totally charming. And many of

Reed's paintings had been sold. It was unlikely he'd ever get his hands on the Lee Eichler Gallery now. Amanda had turned out to have far more guts than he would have ever guessed from her quiet manner.

Dieter ran a red pencil through another line of acid copy. He'd spent hours crafting witty, destructive phrases designed to bring her down. Now he was afraid to use them. His ruddy complexion turned bright red as he struggled to squelch the embarrassing situation with wry humor, but everything he put on paper sounded like sour grapes. He reworked a sentence and then crossed it out, again and again. His poison pen had run completely dry.

Finally, he tore the script in half and yelled at the director. "You can all go home. I'm going to have the program planner rerun the piece I did on Klee." *Amanda will be sorry*, he thought. *Very sorry.*

ຍຉຍຉ

Looking out of her office window, Amanda saw Rudolf drive up in front of the gallery. He pushed past her assistant and into her office, taking a chair opposite her desk. He refused her offer of coffee, so she went right into the events of the previous night.

He looked at the photos of her car. "So you didn't see who hit you and didn't get a license number. I'll take these along to the traffic boys. Next time you have an auto accident, don't call Homicide."

"I thought this attack on me might be related to Marlene's murder."

"I doubt this is linked in any way to Frau Eichler's death." he said "You do seem to be having a trying time here in Germany, Frau Lee. Sometimes, one is better off staying in their own country." He touched the brim of his hat, smirked, and started to walk out.

"Unter Kommissar Rudolf," Amanda called after him. "Has any progress been made in finding Marlene's killer?"

"As you might imagine, that's not something I can discuss." Once more he headed for the door.

"What about Harry Philips, the female impersonator shot at Chez Otto? Has his body been found?"

Rudolf turned abruptly. "I contacted Pass Control. My inquiries show that there never was a Harry Philips. Now, good day, Frau Lee." He turned on his heel and strode through the door.

A few minutes later, Amanda grabbed her coat. "Rolf, I'll be back in an hour or so."

જાજ

Thursday afternoon, he headed for the Gemütlich for a quick beer and lunch. He was surprised to see Amanda Lee get out of a black Porsche and walk quickly toward the restaurant. Her car would be in the shop after the beating it had taken. He hadn't intended to kill her then, just cause a little panic. It was unnerving how much she looked like Marlene—it was like seeing a ghost. He hung back where she couldn't spot him and watched her through the large plate glass window as she spoke to a waiter. What was she doing? Yes, she was showing him a picture. The man left and returned with the manager.

Wait a minute! The manager was nodding his head as he looked at the photo. It must be of Marlene. Men never forgot her beauty, her sexuality. Would they remember her companion? Although he came here occasionally, they really didn't know him. The place was always jammed, making it hard to remember the infrequent customer. It had been possible to stage a cover-up at Chez Otto. Otto would do anything for the right consideration. The male Seglenda was now performing at the bottom of the Rhine. The Bier Halle was a different story. What did she find out? Amanda would have to die and soon.

୧୨୧୨

He clipped two pictures to the top of his easel and selected a fresh canvas. His black eyes looked through narrowed lids at these images as he sketched an outline. His brush worked quickly, merging the important elements of both pictures into a single scene, relying on his imagination for enhancement. He worked feverishly for a couple of hours, trying to accomplish as much as possible before he had to stop and feed the hungry lion of his addiction.

Putting down the palette, he looked at the results so far. *Blood curdling*, he noted with satisfaction.

Walking over to the kitchen area, he reached under the sink for his stash of heroin. An especially large dose was called for to reward himself for work well done. After preparing a syringe, he placed a rubber tube around his arm and pulled it tight. He pierced his gray-white flesh already peppered with scars. Within moments, the drug washed over him with the first pleasant rush. He stared at the unfinished painting. It was even better than the last one. Yes, it was excellent—the vivid colors, the exquisite horror. He continued to admire his work until the drug took full effect, and he sank into what he called "the blessed coma of the undead."

CHAPTER 20

Amanda returned to the gallery still thinking about her discussions with the waiter and the manager of the Gemütlich. They had both recognized the photograph of Marlene at once and recalled she'd been there several times, including the weekend of her death.

"Oh yes," the waiter had said. "I would never forget that face. I remember she was here on a Friday because we only make our famous sauerbraten on Fridays. People come from all over for it. I told her how good it was, even describing the marinade in great detail. Then I realized she wasn't listening, as if she was in another world. She ended up ordering a salad. We had to make it up special because no one comes here for salad."

"Was anyone with her?" Amanda asked.

"A man joined her a few minutes later."

When Amanda asked about Marlene's companion, the waiter described him as tall, blond, and fairly attractive. "I didn't pay a lot of attention to him, I'm afraid. We are always extremely busy on Fridays."

"Are you sure he was blond?" the manager said. "I thought she was with an ordinary-looking man with brown or maybe reddish hair. I remember they were sitting in that booth right over there."

The waiter looked puzzled. "Perhaps we are thinking of two different occasions. Well, maybe you're right. I could be mistaken about the man, but I am sure about the woman."

The Bier Halle accepted no credit cards, so there was no record of the man's name.

If the manager remembered correctly, the lunch companion could well have been Dieter. But a beer hall really wasn't Dieter's style.

On the other hand, the waiter seemed to be certain the man was "blond and attractive." Could be Hans Demuth. Or maybe Wolf had met her for lunch. They did meet occasionally. No, Wolf had been in Amsterdam that weekend. The mysterious lunch companion must have been Demuth. But why would Marlene meet him? To ask him to stop harassing her with those awful phone calls? To try to reason with him? And with his wife's money, he could easily commission a painting.

ⱳⱭⱳⱭ

The shirt laid out on Grutzmacher's desk had splashes of blood down the front. The initials *HD* embroidered on the distinctive custom label had been verified by Hans Demuth's tailor. He said the shirt was one of a dozen he had recently made for Hans. The note that came with the shirt—unsigned of course—said Hans had worn it the night he killed Marlene Eichler.

The postmark was from a station in the wealthiest part of town, near the Demuth home. Flipping the intercom switch, he called for an officer to take the garment to forensics. If this blood matched that of Marlene Eichler, they just might have their killer.

It was six o'clock Thursday evening, and Grutzmacher was tired. As he headed home, he remembered he was out of schnapps. He pulled over and parked near one of the open newsstands that sold papers, magazines, tobacco, and alcohol.

"A bottle of schnapps, please," he told the old man framed by a myriad of magazines hanging from every available space.

He had nothing to read at home; perhaps he would pick up a copy of *Der Stern*. As he reached for the magazine, a feature headline on the cover jumped out at him; *Wolf Eichler—A Star Architect's Private Home.*

❧❧❧

After dinner, Grutzmacher settled into his favorite

easy chair with his schnapps and the magazine. He opened it to the story on Eichler. It had been photographed during the summer, as the gardens were in full bloom. There were several interior shots of the house—one showed Eichler posing in his study. He was seated in a chair next to a distinctively carved mantel. The article said he had designed the furniture to contrast with his historic Jugendstil house. Could this man have murdered his ex-wife? Rudolf certainly thought so, but there was no real evidence against him except those tuxedo studs. Well, they'd have to see what the lab had to say about Demuth's bloody shirt.

∞∞

Friday morning, Hans Demuth lay on the bed in the upstairs guest room staring at the ceiling. He hadn't been to work in days. He'd been avoiding Helga, hoping she'd cool off, but this time was different. She was planning to throw him out. He knew it. He reached for the bottle of vodka on the nightstand and took a big gulp without sitting up. The warm liquid spilled over his lips and ran down the side of his unshaven face onto the fine Swiss linens. He swallowed several times, ignoring the burning sensation as the vodka hit his stomach.

What would become of him? He wasn't fit to do anything except play the role of chief executive. Everyone knew Helga and her top employees made the real decisions. He didn't mind that. He worked very little, enjoyed a high position, and collected a huge salary. Now he'd be a laughing stock, maybe have to leave town. No more custom-tailored clothes, sports cars, or money to burn. Of course, there was a prenuptial agreement with Helga that would give him a small settlement, but that was hardly enough to live on. He'd have to get a real job, but doing what? He emptied the vodka bottle and let it slip to the floor.

A few minutes later, he was retching in the bathroom. Oh God, how could he have been so stupid? Getting involved with Marlene Eichler was the most dangerous thing he'd ever done, but he'd been drawn to her for just that reason. The truth was, she'd never cared for him. He'd given of himself and spent money on her, and in return, she'd hung him out to dry. He still hated her for that.

Now he was on a slippery slope with his wife. Her business partner Amanda had proven the final straw. Helga actually believed he was having an affair with her. The irony was, for once, he was innocent. He retched so hard he thought his stomach would turn inside out. He needed to pull himself together. He had things to do.

∽∾

Amanda picked up the phone on the second ring. "Lee Eichler Gallery."

"Frau Lee, this is Sophia Danielle. I sent you a bill for a Chanel dress purchased by your late business partner. It was the last thing she bought from me before she died. It was never paid for."

"Oh yes," Amanda said, "I'm sorry I haven't gotten back to you. I was busy getting ready for my last show."

"When can I expect your check for three thousand marks?"

"First of all, I'd like to verify that Marlene made the purchase. It's not that I don't believe you, but three thousand marks is a large sum, and I want to make sure there's no mistake. Can you describe the dress for me?"

"Yes, it was black Chanel silk with little spaghetti straps."

"I found no such dress in her closet."

"She bought it, no question," Sophia said, "But if you want to see the sales slip come by my shop. I'll be here till six-thirty."

It was around that time when Amanda drove up in front of the Trella Boutique. Musical chimes announced her entry into the shop. Sophia Danielle came out of the back room to greet her.

"Frau Lee, how nice to see you. Please, sit down. I've just made some espresso. There's champagne if you prefer."

"Espresso will be fine," Amanda said, removing her coat and settling into one of the art deco chairs at the front of the shop. "You've redecorated. It looks lovely."

"Yes, a little change is good for the soul, right?"

Amanda could feel Sophia looking at her gray Jil Sander suit. It was the one Marlene had selected the day of the big makeover. How long ago that seemed.

"That outfit is perfect for you," Sophia said. "I have just received some new things by the same designer if you would like to see them."

"Perhaps another time. Now about your bill." Amanda took the charge slip from Sophia. The boutique logo adorned the top, then a personal account number, Marlene's name, and a brief description of the dress. At the bottom, undeniably, was the flowery scrawl of Marlene's signature. "Do you have any idea what happened to this dress?"

"I'm afraid not. It was altered, and she picked it up herself instead of having it delivered."

There was no mistake. Marlene had made the purchase. It was only fair to pay this debt. To Sophia's visible relief, Amanda took out her checkbook and paid the three thousand marks. As she got up to leave, she saw it—the painting of a woman staring longingly out of a window. At first, it appeared to be an original, but as she inspected it more closely, she realized it was an excellent copy of an Edward Hopper. The brushwork, the technique, the intensity of color were exactly the same as in Marlene's death painting. The work was unsigned. "Where did you get this?"

"I bought it in Berlin several years ago," Sophia said.

"Do you remember the name of the artist or the gallery?"

"It came from a funny little place near the zoo. I can't recall the name."

"Can we take a look on the back?"

"Of course." Sophia removed the canvas from the wall, laid it face down on the table, and carefully lifted the protective backing. In one corner was a yellowed sticker. It read *Tiergarten Galerie, Bismarckstrasse, Berlin. Telefon 6213 059.* "Oh yes," Sophia said. "I remember now."

Amanda took out her address book. Her hand trembled as she copied down the information. This painting would lead to the killer. She was sure of it.

"Why do you want the gallery's name?" Sophia said. "It's only a copy."

"I'm interested in the artist. He shows great promise," Amanda said. "Ciao, Sophia, and thank you."

☙❧❧

It was almost dawn. Every star had been extinguished, and gray clouds now smudged the sky outside the windows of his loft.

He stood back for a moment and looked at the work—a thrill stirred in his groin, causing him to get an erection. The woman portrayed was beautiful. He ran his eyes over the contours of her face and the graceful line of her throat. Her soft blonde hair fell like a ribbon over her forehead and echoed the curve of her cheek. Her body was delicious, clad in silky black. Her eyes, half closed and unseeing, had surrendered to the ultimate experience. He had won out over her smugness, over all she had done to him. He'd expertly blended her likeness with the location pictured in the photo. His breathing grew fast and shallow.

A short time later, he heard three short knocks on the door. He wiped the paint off of his hands and admitted his guest. "Come in, it's finished."

CHAPTER 21

Amanda got to work early Saturday morning. Excitement gripped her stomach as she dialed the number she'd jotted down at Sophia's. Maybe the gallery wasn't there anymore. After many rings, the phone was answered. "Guten Morgen, Tiergarten Galerie." The voice sounded like that of a very old man.

"Good morning," Amanda said. "I happened to see a painting purchased from your gallery a few years ago by Sophia Danielle of Cologne. It has no signature, but it's an excellent copy of an Edward Hopper. I was wondering if you had any others by the same artist."

"We sell many copies of well-known artists. Edward Hopper, you say? I haven't had any of those for some time. They were popular a few years ago after the big Hopper shows in Düsseldorf and Berlin. Not much call for them now."

"Do you have any record of who the artist might be?"

"What? What did you say?"

"Could you give me a name?" Amanda's voice rose. "The artist who copies Hopper."

"Oh. Let me see. Could you hold a moment?" Amanda heard a clunk as the phone was put down. She was left hanging so long she thought the old man had forgotten her. At last, he came back on the line. "Hallo. Hallo."

"I'm still here. Any luck?"

"I looked through my records. We had two artists who did Edward Hopper. One of them was a man named Steffen Fischer. The other one, wait…I'm having difficulty making it out. It looks like Klaus something. Yes, Klaus K. Kruger."

So it was Kruger. That sniveling little—

"Hallo, hallo. Are you still there?"

"Yes. Thank you. You've been very helpful."

She sat sculpture still, eyes closed, fists clenched. But why would he want to kill Marlene? She'd been willing to show his work and was even enthusiastic about it. He knew Amanda only agreed because of Marlene. It made no sense for him to get rid of her. No. Kruger must have been commissioned to paint that work, but by whom? Dieter? But why? He also benefited from Kruger's shows. It must have been Hans Demuth. There had to be a way to find out.

First, she wanted to speak to Wolf, tell him of her discovery, and get his input. "Wolf Eichler Associates."

"May I speak to Herr Eichler, please?"

"I'm sorry, meine dame, Herr Eichler is away and cannot be reached at the moment. Is there something I can do?"

"No. I'll call back." She dialed Grutzmacher's number and was relieved when he answered the phone himself.

ৎৡৎ

Grutzmacher was thrilled to finally have a break in the Eichler case. First, he visited the boutique and took the painting as evidence from an astonished Sophia Danielle. Then he spoke to the owner of the Tiergarten Galerie. It was all as Frau Lee had said. Of course, they would run tests to compare paint samples to the death painting, but there was enough here to warrant taking Kruger in for questioning.

The winter sun was bright as he rode to the warehouse district with Ernst Rudolf. The unter kommissar was unusually quiet.

"Pull up over here. We'll walk the rest of the way. I don't want him to see us coming and take off." Grutzmacher indicated a spot next to an ancient bridge guarded by a pair of stone mermaids. The temperature was colder near the water, and the air was filled with the tangy smell of the Rhine. "Let's approach from the back of the building," he said, whispering even though there was no one to overhear them.

Within minutes, they entered the old warehouse where Kruger had his loft and crept up the stairs. When they reached the door, they stood listening for movement inside. There was none.

At Grutzmacher's signal, Rudolf pounded on the door. "Open up, this is the police."

Grutzmacher strained to hear any sound.

"Maybe he's not in there," Rudolf said.

"We have a warrant. Let's go in and find out." Rudolf gave the door a powerful kick. It opened easily; too easily. An empty easel stood before them like an exotic bird with colorful plumage of flecked paint. Grutzmacher half expected it to let out a series of wild shrieks as they intruded upon its odd sanctuary. The loft was cold and damp, unwarmed by shafts of light pouring in through the skylights. Lined up against one wall were various paintings portraying the anguish of the dead and dying.

While Rudolf checked the bathroom, Grutzmacher looked in the kitchenette partially concealed behind a screen. The sink contained a dirty glass and a cup. On the counter was a bottle of Russian vodka two-thirds empty. Its excellent quality was in marked contrast to everything else in the loft. Next to it was a spoon, some matches, and a filthy dishtowel. A plastic garbage can overflowed with takeout cartons, paper plates, and half-eaten food.

"Nothing in the bathroom," Rudolf said, entering the kitchen. "Anything of interest in here?"

Grutzmacher indicated the vodka. They walked back into the main part of the loft. Almost simultaneously both men were drawn to the mattress lying on the floor. The soiled comforter was twisted into lumps over what appeared to be a mass of tangled sheets.

A pillow stuck out at one end. Rudolf leaned down and grabbed a corner of the comforter, giving it a swift yank. The body of Klaus K. Kruger appeared like an evil wraith, his skull-like head facing toward them and staring with near-colorless eyes; the mouth gaped open in a silent scream. There was a piece of tubing tied round one bony arm. Just beneath, sticking deep into the flesh, was a syringe. The skin around it was yellow and blue from hemorrhaging.

Grutzmacher knelt beside the body. "My God."

"He looks like one of his own paintings," Rudolf said.

"Yes. I've always believed that whatever we dwell on in our minds eventually manifests in our lives, good or evil."

"Obviously a drug overdose," Rudolf said.

"Maybe, maybe not. Look at the syringe. It appears to have been stabbed into his arm. No one inserts a needle that deep, especially someone experienced."

"If he drank most of that vodka before he decided to shoot up, he could have fallen while administering the drug. That would account for the fact that it went in more deeply. It's an OD, pure and simple."

"Nothing is ever pure and simple." Grutzmacher removed a pair of latex gloves from his pocket and pulled them on. He ran his fingers over the face, along the neck, and down the chest and body. "Rigor has already set in." He carefully turned Kruger over. He was wearing only his leather pants, so his back was visible. And purple. The skin blotched wherever Grutzmacher's fingers pressed in. "The color is not yet permanent. Judging from the advancement of the rigor and the lividity, he has probably been dead about three to four hours."

Rudolf looked at his watch. "It is ten o'clock now. That would make the time of death around six or seven this morning."

"Yes. Lipke can give us a more accurate timing." The kommissar returned the corpse to its original position. He lifted one of Kruger's hands. "There's wet paint under his fingernails. He must have been working on something new." Grutzmacher got up, walked over to the easel, and touched a glob of bright red paint. "Still wet." Kruger's palette lay on a metal cabinet next to the easel. "He was using bright colors."

He did a quick check of the paintings against the wall. "Where's the new work?"

"Must be one of those," Rudolph said.

"No, the palette has a completely different color spectrum from these, which feature muted tones, and they are dry. The new one would still be wet."

"Maybe he started something, didn't like it, and threw it out."

"Threw it out...where? He didn't bother to throw out the garbage. I doubt he would throw away a canvas. Put a call in to Lipke and the crime scene unit. Be sure they put top priority on the lab tests." Grutzmacher paused. "I'll take another look in the kitchen."

Once more, he stepped behind the screen. Still wearing gloves, he carefully picked up the pricey bottle of vodka. It looked to him like Kruger had entertained a visitor just prior to his death.

ဢၜၜ

At eight p.m. Grutzmacher entered the cold gray of the autopsy room. Kruger's naked body lay on a large stainless-steel table with raised sides and a drain at one end. A scale hung beside the table. Kruger's eyes were now closed, but he did not look peaceful. His face wore the tortured expression of a soul in hell. Lipke selected a scalpel from a tray of instruments. He examined it for a moment with his large, frog-like eyes then turned to Grutzmacher. "Ready, Fredrich?"

ဢၜၜ

By Sunday night the television news was full of Kruger's death. "Drug overdose, self-inflicted was the official conclusion of Uwe Lipke, the Cologne medical examiner."

The forensics report confirmed that there was only one set of fingerprints on the vodka bottle and the glass—Kruger's—and that his were also the only prints on the syringe.

In spite of that, Grutzmacher believed Kruger had been murdered. There was enough heroin in his system to have killed him several times. It was not likely he would make that kind of mistake. Vodka was found in his stomach but only a small amount. Rudolph's theory was that Kruger had purchased the vodka himself and consumed it over time.

It appeared to Grutzmacher that someone else had brought it to Kruger's loft, and he drank it to be companionable with his visitor, who must have had the lion's share—perhaps a celebration of some sort. But of what? The new painting he'd been working on? Where was it now? Forensics was testing red pigment taken from Kruger's easel against those of Frau Eichler's death painting and the one taken from Sofia Danielli. Even before the official report, Grutzmacher was certain that they would match.

He lit a cigarette and waited for results from the lab. Rudolf had left the building long ago. Around midnight, an official document was placed on his desk, and he scanned the results.

Now, what Grutzmacher wanted to know was why

Dieter Becker, Germany's leading art authority, had failed to realize that the artist whom he had sponsored was the same artist they'd been seeking in the Eichler case. He needed to have a serious conversation with Herr Becker. He'd call in the morning.

∽∾∽

Amanda picked up the phone and dialed Demuth's office. "I'm sorry, but Herr Demuth is out sick today."

She hung up and dialed again.

"Demuth residence."

"May I speak with Herr Demuth?"

"I'll see if he's in. Whom shall I say is calling?"

"Amanda Lee." Amanda's nerves were on edge. The plan she had in mind was hastily conceived, but she was sure it would work. "Hans Demuth here."

"Herr Demuth, I need to speak to you face to face."

"I don't believe we have anything to say to each other."

"Oh, but we do. I have evidence that you killed Marlene Eichler."

"Don't be ridiculous."

"I have proof that it was you. I'm willing to forget all about it if you'll pay me a reasonable sum to cover the trauma all this has caused me." Amanda's heart was banging against her ribs, but her voice was steady.

"You must be mad."

"You won't think so when the police knock on your door."

"What proof do you have?"

"I'll meet you tonight at the Gemütlich Bier Halle at eight o'clock. If you fail to show up, I'll give my evidence to Grutzmacher."

∽∾∽

The hall phone sounded like a siren warning of impending danger. Dieter had left word at the office that he was taking a few days off. He had drunk himself into a coma the previous night. It was only ten in the morning, and he was already half drunk again and didn't want to speak to anyone. The incessant ringing stopped, only to start again a few minutes later.

"Becker here."

"Good morning, Dieter. This is Fredrich Grutzmacher. As you may know, we found the body of Klaus Kruger yesterday."

"Yes, yes. I heard it on the news. It's a shame, a real shame."

"Could you come over here and clear up a few matters for us?"

"What, now? I'm not well today, Fredrich. Perhaps tomorrow. I seem to have caught some kind of bug an—"

"Then I'll come to you. See you in a bit."

"But, Fredrich, I'm not—"

The phone was dead. Grutzmacher was already on his way. Dieter looked at himself in the hall mirror. His eyes, his face, and his tousled hair were various shades of red. He'd better pull himself together.

⌀⌀⌀

When Grutzmacher called Dieter's office, he had asked for his home address as well as the telephone number. He was surprised to learn Dieter lived in Düsseldorf instead of Cologne. In fact, he lived in the same luxurious part of town as Wolf Eichler. It was about a forty-five-minute drive. The kommissar went alone. Rudolf and his overzealous tactics only got in the way of this type of interview.

He finally located the right street. It was lined with impressive homes on large pieces of property. The three-story stone house on the cul-de-sac must have once been as grand as the others. Now it had fallen into disrepair, barely visible behind a tangle of overgrown shrubs and trees. A tall, rusting iron fence surrounded the property. The gate complained loudly when it was opened. This must be Dieter's family home. Why had he let it sink to such a state? Grutzmacher rang the bell, and the door opened immediately.

"Come in, Fredrich, come in."

A small transom window let a square of feeble light into the hallway. As he entered the house, Grutzmacher was immediately struck by the smell of mildew and of general neglect. He smelled alcohol on Dieter.

"Forgive the appearance of my humble home. I don't have a housekeeper. Can't abide them." Dieter, in striped pajamas and flannel robe, looked as if he hadn't slept all night. He coughed and cleared his throat. "I am sorry to greet you this way, my friend."

Adjacent to the front door was a grand staircase covered with faded red carpeting. At the top of the stairs, a life-sized portrait of an attractive redhead looked down on them with an imperious gaze.

Dieter bowed toward it in an elaborate gesture of introduction. "My mother."

"She was a very beautiful woman. Is this the family home?"

"While she lived, it was my mother's house. She ruled it like a queen. A speck of dust was tantamount to treason."

"I take it she had a housekeeper," Grutzmacher said, stepping over a pile of old magazines, as he followed Dieter into the living room.

"Oh, yes. Servants cleaning and polishing all day long. It literally drove me crazy."

The room was dark—made more so by the mahogany wall paneling, heavy drapery, and pieces of antique furniture. Strips of peeling paint hung precariously from the ceiling like large moths ready to take flight. Years of stains decorated the oriental rug.

"Evolutionists," Dieter said, "say that man is descended from the great apes. It is my contention that our natures are the issue of the great swine. We only engage in the ritual of cleaning to make ourselves acceptable to one another. Without the judgments of society, we would be content to wallow in our own filth."

"An interesting theory." Grutzmacher removed a pile of clothing from a tapestry-covered love seat and sat down.

"Now, Fredrich, to what do I owe this honor?"

"I'm making routine inquiries into the death of Klaus Kruger."

"Really?" Dieter walked over to the bar and poured himself a stiff vodka. "Breakfast! Would you like one? Of course not, you're on duty. Well, I'm not, and I doubt very much if I've fooled you into thinking I am in this condition because of the flu. I've been working very hard lately, and I needed to take it easy for a day or so." He raised his glass in Grutzmacher's direction and sat down in a large chair opposite the love seat. "Right. Klaus Kruger. What do you want to know?"

"You were the one who discovered him as an artist, am I correct? Exactly where and when did you first meet him?"

"In Berlin about a year and a half ago. I was writing a series of articles on street artists." Dieter downed the vodka. "The poor bugger was hustling tourists with copies of masterpieces while trying to develop his own style."

"Did you happen to notice which painters he copied?"

"Oh, Miro, Kandinsky—I don't remember them all."

"What about Edward Hopper?"

"Hopper? Mmmm...I don't think so." Dieter walked over to a window and opened the drapery.

"You were unaware that he did copies of Hopper's work for the Tiergarten Galerie?"

Dieter was silent for a moment then turned and faced Grutzmacher. "For my article, I was only interested in his life on the street. How he survived, who bought his work, that sort of thing. And no, I didn't know of his affiliation with any gallery at that time."

"What attracted you to Kruger?"

"I suppose it was his paintings portraying death. Many great artists have chosen death as a subject. His work showed an intensity that stood out. I thought he had potential."

"Did you advise him to come to Cologne?"

"He did that on his own. After his arrival, he contacted me and invited me to his loft to view his new works. I went and was impressed with his progress from the year before."

"And you decided he should have a one-man show at the Lee Eichler Gallery?"

"I might have mentioned it to Marlene."

"How well did you know Frau Eichler?"

"We knew each other for many years. I was very fond of her."

"So you arranged a big show for Kruger, televised it, and wrote about him in your column."

"Right you are, Fredrich." Dieter went back to the bar and poured himself another vodka, spilling a little on the rug.

"I am wondering why, with your knowledge of Kruger's work, you didn't realize that it was Kruger who created Frau Eichler's death painting."

Dieter stopped in mid-sip. "You must be mistaken."

"No mistake. We have indisputable evidence."

"I know Kruger was a strange duck, but I find what you've just told me to be unbelievable," Dieter said, lowering himself into the chair. "What could his motive have been? Do you know?"

"I thought perhaps you might shed some light on that subject. Did he have any disagreements with Frau Eichler that you're aware of?"

"No. In fact, she acted more or less as his benefactress by showing his work. It's the kind of thing the more established galleries wouldn't touch. There is no reason that I know of for him to kill Marlene."

"Perhaps he was not the killer. Perhaps he was only commissioned to do the painting. Do you know who might commission such a work?"

"No."

"Weren't you a good friend of Herr Kruger?"

"Absolutely not. I thought he had some talent, that's all. I frequently promote an artist whom I personally dislike. It's the art that's important."

"I see. Was Kruger's show at the Lee Eichler gallery successful?"

"Yes. Unfortunately, when Frau Lee took over after Marlene's death, she dropped Kruger immediately."

"Did he harbor resentment against Frau Lee?"

"What do you think? I was none too happy about it myself. A lot of money was lost. I planned to help him find another gallery as soon as he got a new show together."

"But his addiction got in the way."

"He was a drug addict. Nevertheless, he kept working. It was undoubtedly the drugs that helped him envision the divine horror he painted."

"So he wasn't a personal friend of yours?"

"No. I've already told you our relationship was that of critic and artist."

"Then why did you give him large sums of money on a regular basis dating from the time he arrived in Cologne?"

"What? I—I didn't."

"Don't bother to deny it, Dieter. Before coming here this morning, I contacted your bank. Withdrawals from your account over the last months match perfectly with deposits into Kruger's account." Grutzmacher studied

Dieter's face. The cockiness was gone. He looked old, tired, and defeated. "Why would you give him such sums of money?"

"I…well, I was just helping him out. He was broke, and I was helping him survive until he had his big show, that's all. I have nothing more to say to you, Fredrich. I would like you to leave my house now."

CHAPTER 22

It was almost eight p.m. Amanda had arrived at the Gemütlich Bier Halle fifteen minutes early. She was surprised to see how different the place was at night. The waiter and the helpful manager she'd met on her previous visit were not there. She had hoped they would be. She'd have felt more secure.

Instead, a rather dour-looking man in a long white apron came from behind the bar and showed her to a booth next to the window. He placed a menu in her hand and walked away without saying a word. Dim lighting permeated the restaurant area, with an island of brighter light at the bar. Instead of the cheerful, workaday lunch crowd of young men and women, there was a mostly older male clientele gathered around the bar. They sat on bar stools discussing soccer, sometimes looking up at a television set that had the volume turned down to a low hum.

Rain the color of tarnished silver slid down the large plate glass window. Amanda could see the street outside was almost deserted, except for one or two pedestrians concealed beneath black umbrellas and the occasional car swishing through puddles on the wet cobblestones.

This table allowed her to watch who was coming and going. She had it all worked out in her mind. She would tell Demuth that before Kruger died, she'd made a deal to give him another show in exchange for his revealing who'd hired him to do the death painting. When he told her it was the very wealthy Herr Demuth, she decided it was better justice for Marlene, as well as more profitable for herself, if she made a deal asking for DM 20,000 in exchange for her silence. Being an unscrupulous person himself, he'd probably believe the same of her. She knew he was highly motivated to keep any hint of scandal from his wife. Then, if he offered to give her the money—and she was certain he would—she'd know he was Marlene's killer and go to the police. She could prove her allegations by picking up the money wearing a wire so that the police could hear Demuth's guilt for themselves. Unquestionable proof even the cynical Ernst Rudolf could not dispute. What a relief it would be to have it all over with. For a moment, her thoughts drifted to Wolf, the one good to come out of all this.

Amanda sipped white wine and looked repeatedly at her watch. Choosing a public place gave her a certain amount of security. She had picked up the Porsche earlier, restored to its former glory and with a car phone newly installed. If there was any funny business on the way home, she could call for help.

The clock over the bar said eight-fifteen, the same as her watch. Maybe he was delayed by the weather. It was due to get worse as the night wore on. The waiter approached her, pad and pencil in hand, but she just smiled and shook her head. Eight-thirty. Eight-forty-five—where was he? She became vaguely aware of a tapping sound—and realized it was the sound of her own fingernails on the table's surface. Nine o'clock, still no Demuth.

One by one, the group of macho patrons in the Bier Halle dwindled. "Going to have sleet in a few hours. Better head out early before the roads ice over," said the last burly beer drinker as he pushed some marks across the bar. The man in the white apron nodded. He once again approached Amanda.

"We are closing now."

She left her wine unfinished and paid the check.

As soon as Amanda stepped outside, the restaurant's lighted sign went out above her. The rain, turning to sleet, looked like a curtain of crystal beads. It clattered against her umbrella, the street, and the car—the only sound filling the dark void of night.

Straining her eyes, she looked in both directions. No sign of Demuth or anyone else.

❧❧❧

Hans Demuth's face was filled with anguish as he looked at the bloody shirt and the note lying on Grutzmacher's desk. "I didn't kill Marlene, I swear it." It was nine p.m. Grutzmacher poured two cups of coffee and handed one to Demuth. He needed it. The man was a mess—disheveled clothing, a three-day growth of beard, and he'd obviously had been drinking heavily.

"Then why would someone accuse you in this manner?"

"I don't know. I—wait. It must have been my wife, Helga. She is the only one with access to my clothing. Damn her for this."

"Why would she go to such lengths?" Grutzmacher asked.

"I had an affair with Marlene Eichler, and Helga suspected I was having another with Amanda Lee. She began having me followed by a private detective. He must have given my wife the mistaken idea that I was romantically involved with Frau Lee."

"So you think this was done out of revenge." Grutzmacher almost pitied Demuth.

"Yes, yes! Please believe me. The blood on that shirt is not Marlene's."

"The forensics team is running tests. We'll know soon enough. If this blood is not Frau Eichler's, whose blood is it, may I ask?"

"It's mine. I bumped my nose in a silly car accident with our next-door neighbors. At first, there were just a few drops, but by the time I got inside the house, my nose was pouring blood. I threw the shirt into the laundry basket to be washed."

Grutzmacher believed him. He didn't think a man this weak would have the stomach for murder, especially one as grotesque as Frau Eichler's.

"Do you know who might have wanted to kill Frau Eichler?"

"Any number of people."

"Can you be a little more specific."

"Wolf Eichler, for one. She was obsessed with him—never let him alone. I don't know how I could have deluded myself that she really cared about me when all she talked about was him."

෴

Wolf was so furious, his anger could be felt over the phone. "Amanda, how many times must I tell you? Stop trying to handle this alone.

"All right, Wolf. I just thought that if I could get Demuth to admit what he did, then go to the police—"

"I know, my love, but last night you deliberately placed yourself in harm's way. If you had been killed, this man would still be free, and I would have lost you forever." His voice softened. "Look, I have an idea. Why don't you move in with me until all this is cleared up."

"I couldn't—I—"

"My house is secure, and I will be there at night to protect you."

"But Wolf, my business is in Cologne, and—"

"I will not take no for an answer. There is a fast train between Düsseldorf and Cologne that will get you to the gallery in twenty-five minutes."

"What about my little cat, Regen? I can't leave him behind. Rolf lives in a rooming house, so he can't keep him."

"Bring him. Just move in. Today is not soon enough."

"I have some things to take care of at the gallery, so it'll be Friday evening before I can be there."

"As you wish. And, Amanda, I think it's safer if you don't discuss this with anyone. Anna is off on the weekends, so she will not be there when you arrive. I have a meeting in Amsterdam that morning, so I may be late. Someone from my office will bring you a set of keys. Just let yourself in."

CHAPTER 23

Ernst Rudolf picked up the paper and unlocked the door of his apartment. It was a one-room affair over a noisy bar. Most of the time the noise didn't bother him. It was three o'clock, and he was letting himself off a little early today. He'd told Grutzmacher he was still checking into the murder case at the farmer's market. Some fool Turkish vegetable seller had gotten himself shot by a robber. He'd nosed around the crime scene for a while and then left the forensics team to do the rest. Unlike the old man, he saw no need to oversee everything personally.

And what did it matter if one more foreigner was killed? There were too many of them in Germany as it was. Germany should be for the Germans, not the beggars who crossed the borders daily, looking to gorge themselves on unearned prosperity.

Good riddance to one more leech.

He pulled off his boots and put them in the closet. Walking in his stocking feet to the fridge, he grabbed a beer and opened it before falling onto his neatly made bed with the newspaper. He surveyed his domain—an old dresser, a chair, and a TV were pushed against the walls of the room. The small kitchenette was right next to the bathroom. There was a standing wardrobe for his immaculate uniforms and the few leisure clothes he had. A metal military chest held private things such as his journals, photographs, and souvenirs of the memorable events in his life. He should have better than this, and very soon he would.

He scanned the front page of the paper. The idiots in the Bundestag were busy making even more liberal laws to help the underprivileged. Couldn't they see these laws were only for the benefit of outsiders?

He turned to the local news. There was a picture of Klaus Kruger's funeral. The minister looking appropriately holy, Klaus's frumpy aunt trying to appear sad, and yes, there was Grutzmacher and he, himself. He looked pretty good—handsome and authoritative.

Too bad about Klaus. The two of them went back all the way to middle school, a couple of troublemakers who'd lived by their wits. Klaus had acted as a reminder to Rudolf of just how far he'd come since the old days. Unfortunately, his drug-loving friend had been asking to die as he did.

A two-line item about the Eichler case appeared at the end of the local news section. "*Marlene Eichler's death is still under investigation, and several lines of inquiry are being pursued. Police will not release any further information at this time, according to Polizeikommissar Fredrich Grutzmacher.*"

Soon Grutzmacher would be sent out to pasture where he belonged, and Rudolf would become a *polizeikommissar*. He hated that Grutzmacher cramped his style. He had already started rumors that the man was getting too old and too soft for the job. He knew how to place a well-timed word here and there that created doubt and filtered up to the top brass. He couldn't wait to see Grutzmacher's face when he, Rudolf, solved the Eichler case.

After taking a long pull on the sweating beer bottle, he turned to the social page. There was a photo of a society ball held for some stupid benefit or other. If there was one thing he hated more than the poor, sniveling immigrants, it was the German upper class. What a worthless lot they were. Very soon he would strike a blow that would send them all reeling. He'd use that American woman to produce all the evidence anyone would need that Eichler had murdered his former wife and his housekeeper. Rudolf put down the paper and picked up a pen and his journal. It was important to record his thoughts daily. It helped him to evaluate things.

CHAPTER 24

Friday morning, Amanda downed the last of her coffee and opened the back door to let little Regen out into the walled garden. The sun shone in a pale blue sky, promising a glorious day. She took deep breaths of the crisp, cold air. It felt good to be alive.

She ran upstairs to pack her suitcase. Now she was excited about moving in with Wolf. He'd called to say they had reservations for Saturday night at the Blaue Maler, a lovely restaurant overlooking the Rhine. Afterward, they'd attend the ballet *Swan Lake*. Tonight, she looked forward to their quiet evening at home. She could almost feel Wolf's arms around her as she placed a champagne colored nightgown and matching robe on top of her other clothes.

It was past nine a.m. Amanda hurriedly slipped into black cashmere pants and sweater. Which coat? In the back of the closet was Marlene's lustrous black mink. As she wrapped it around herself, she could almost hear Marlene say, "Mink is so practical—it goes with everything."

She scooped up little Regen and put him in his carrier. They would leave from the gallery. "We'll have a new home for a little while," she told him. "I think you'll like it."

ఌఄఌ

The mantel clock was striking ten a.m. when Dieter woke up. Thank God he was still on leave from the newspaper. He lay for a while, making out faces and animal shapes in the shadows on the ceiling. It was time to sell this old place and get away from his mother once and for all. Maybe he would buy a condo in one of those new towers they were building near his work.

As a child, he'd had dreams of becoming a great artist and would spend hours in the attic creating his "masterpieces." It was his only refuge from his mother's constant belittling. He could still hear her screaming "You have no talent," and "You're not normal," and "I'm ashamed to call you my son."

He'd hated her and wished her dead many times. He could still see her, after he escaped the institution and came home, berating him as she descended the main staircase. She tripped on her dressing gown and fell headlong down the entire flight. Dieter could tell by the odd position of her head that her neck was broken. She stared at him in death as she had in life, with cold unfeeling eyes. Accusations of having pushed her and once again being institutionalized almost broke him.

Dieter rolled over on his side and looked out the small arched window. Even through the dirty glass, he saw it was a beautiful day. As he started to get out of bed, he heard a crunching sound. He'd fallen asleep on top of the file labeled *Confidential—Property of the Düssldorf Psychiatrisch Anstalt*.

No one would ever threaten him with this again. Kruger's aunt turned out to have been one of his caretakers in the youth ward. Apparently, she never forgot him or the indignities he'd suffered. Because of his family's prominence, she knew that stealing his file would pay off one day. Then Kruger moved to Cologne, and the two of them started blackmailing him. He couldn't let them make that scandal public and ruin his career, his entire life—so he paid. Promoting Kruger's work had also been part of the deal. Now Kruger was dead, his dear auntie had been scared off, and Dieter had the file. He was free at last.

He picked up the folder and walked to the hall stairs. When he reached the bottom, he turned and looked up at the portrait of his mother. He would donate it to the museum she had loved so much.

He went into the living room and placed the file in

the fireplace, sprinkled it with brandy, and struck a match.

 ❧❧❧

The late afternoon sun streamed into the conference room, giving the eight men sitting around the table an almost spiritual glow.

"The permanent collection will be housed in a series of geodesic domes of varying heights and levels joined by archways…" Wolf continued his presentation to nods of approval.

Outside, Amsterdam was turning into the shades of gold and cerulean blue that had inspired Van Gogh. Wolf hurried along the crowded streets toward where he'd garaged his car. There would be a little breather while the building committee considered his presentation. He thought of Amanda. He was glad he'd convinced her to move in with him. It made things so much easier. A tingle of excitement danced over his skin. He couldn't wait to get home.

 ❧❧❧

At six o'clock, Amanda locked the gallery and went out to her car. She listened to Mozart as she turned onto the Autobahn heading in the direction of Düsseldorf. Around noon, a messenger had arrived carrying a box from Cartier. It contained a key placed on a platinum ring with a charm engraved with her initials and accented with a blue sapphire.

Traffic was moderate, and she made it to Düsseldorf in under an hour. Soon she was on the Rathausufer, a twisting avenue that made its way along the Rhine. It was lined with evenly spaced Japonais trees. Their dark straight trunks topped with gnarled branches gave them the appearance of ancient sentinels in heavy headdresses. As she looked out at the black waters, a tugboat was slowly moving downriver, its lights dimmed by fog. Its horn pierced the night, emitting a lonely bray.

Just ahead was the bridge that crossed over to the wealthy Oberkassel part of town. A few minutes later, she turned into the curved driveway that led to Wolf's house. Dense shrubbery shielded the property from the street. He was not home yet. Everything was dark except for a lighted walkway obviously on a timer.

Amanda took her suitcase and Regen and headed for the front door. A few seconds later, she was inside the hallway where a sconce had been left on, bathing the organic décor and delicately curved staircase in a romantic glow.

"I'll let you out in a minute," she told the cat as she set down his carrier. After putting her coat away in the hall closet, she took Regen into the kitchen, fed him, and closed the door. It was best to confine him to one room until he felt more at home.

She took her things up to the guest room. She knew she wouldn't be sleeping there, but she wanted to hang up her clothes and unpack her toiletries. She freshened her makeup, ran a brush through her hair, and dabbed on a little Blue Iris perfume. It was going to be a wonderful weekend.

Now to make a fire in the study so things will be warm and inviting when Wolf arrives. As she entered the room, her happy mood slowly melted into a strange unease. The kindling and wood had already been laid in the fireplace.

Soon, leaping flames changed the large room into a contrast of darting light and deep, moving shadows. Although she heard nothing but the crackling fire, she sensed a presence. "Wolf? Wolf, is that you? Come out, come out wherever you are."

Her words disappeared in the silence of the house like pebbles tossed into a deep well. He wasn't home yet; his car wasn't in the driveway. He wouldn't play games with her, not after all that had happened.

As she looked around, she noticed an easel in the corner holding a large painting. The work was covered by a piece of muslin. It was too dim to see well, so she turned on the overhead lamp. A beam of light poured onto the canvas as she removed the covering.

She suppressed an urge to vomit as her stomach clenched. There in front of her, in the style of Edward Hopper, was her own death painting. It portrayed Amanda isolated and alone, abandoned by life. The artist had captured her likeness in this very room, tied to the straight-backed chair by the fireplace. She wore a figure-hugging black dress with spaghetti straps. There were bloody knife wounds to her arms and legs, the torn flesh revealed by gashes in the dress. Her head lolled against the tall back of the chair. Like Marlene, her throat had been cut. Amanda shut her eyes tight, unwilling to confront what she knew was waiting behind her.

"Good evening, Amanda. I think it is a very good likeness, don't you?"

CHAPTER 25

It was seven-thirty p.m. Grutzmacher was still at his desk mulling over the facts in the Eichler case. Demuth had been eliminated as a suspect. The blood on his shirt was his own. They'd also located the bar where he'd been the night of Marlene's murder. His obnoxious behavior was well remembered by the bartender. He had been there, passed out, until the bar closed at one a.m.

What about Dieter Becker? Grutzmacher just couldn't see Dieter as a killer, especially after the scene in his home. He might have suspected Kruger did the death painting, although he said he did not. For Dieter to murder Marlene didn't make sense. With her alive, he had a guaranteed venue for any talent he wished to promote. Still, it was puzzling why he would give money to Kruger.

That left Wolf Eichler. It was possible he murdered

his wife. He certainly had motive, and his alibi was anything but airtight. He could still have keys to the condo
since he lived there with Marlene after they were married.
Eichler was a collector; he might have met Kruger at a
show, offered him money to do the painting, then killed
him to keep him quiet. This was Rudolf's theory and it
did have merit. But why do the painting at all? How did
Amanda Lee fit into all of this? Was she an accomplice to
Eichler? They have been seen together a lot lately.

Grutzmacher reached up and rubbed the space between his eyebrows. He swiveled his chair to look down
at the Rhine. Instead of it having the usual relaxing effect,
he found the scene unsettling. The river was cloaked in a
heavy fog. The swirling vapors rose from the river and
pressed against the window like tortured souls. A sense of
impending doom descended on him.

He got up and moved away from the window. He
was just tired, that's all. This unsolved case was weighing
on him. It was time to go home, get some rest. He pulled
on his trench coat and headed down the hallway. There
were only a couple of officers in the squad room, drinking coffee and reliving the previous night's soccer game.

He turned the corner and entered the empty corridor
that led past Rudolf's office. The unter kommissar
seemed to have been avoiding Grutzmacher during the
past week. It had reached him only this morning that Rudolph was spreading the word throughout the department
that the "old man" was a hindrance to the Eichler investi-

gation. When it was solved, Rudolf would be the one to solve it, and he was close to doing so. It infuriated him that men he had worked with for years would pay any attention to this brash upstart.

As he came to Rudolf's office, on impulse, he went in. He closed the door, pulled the blinds, and switched on the green-shaded desk lamp. Everything was obsessively tidy—pens, files, and notes put away with compulsive neatness.

He opened the top drawer and found it filled with the usual paper clips, various police forms, and rubber stamps. The second drawer contained notebooks of the cases Rudolf was working on. Grutzmacher looked through them. The Eichler casebook was missing. He tried the bottom drawer. Locked. He hesitated for a moment. An unexplained anxiety continued to build in his gut. He took out his penknife, and, a moment later, the drawer slid open. Inside, there was a stack of police gazettes. Why would anyone lock up these things? Grutzmacher glanced at the one on top. The cover showed a picture of an unter kommissar from Munich. The headline read, *Officer of the Month*. The article inside explained how this man, "with diligence and courage," solved a case that had been on the books for over a year. There were lots of grisly photographs. Perhaps Rudolf pictured himself on a cover some day.

Grutzmacher lifted out the stack of journals. Beneath them was the Eichler casebook. He leafed through Rudolf's notes. Nothing he didn't already know. As he started to put it back into the drawer, a white envelope fluttered to the floor. Inside was a photograph and a magazine page smudged with red paint, the same blood red shade he'd seen in Kruger's studio the day they had discovered his body. The photo was of Amanda Lee, a full-length shot taken on the street, clearly without her knowledge. The magazine page was from *Der Stern's* feature on Wolf Eichler and showed the distinctive fireplace in his home. Fear gripped Grutzmacher's heart. Kruger had been using these to create a death painting of Frau Lee, similar to the one of Marlene Eichler. That must have been the painting he was working on just before he died—the one they couldn't find.

Rudolf must have found the pictures during their search of Kruger's loft, recognized their significance, and withheld them to solve the crime himself and play the big hero. By withholding this evidence, he had placed Frau Lee in grave danger.

Where was the painting now? Eichler must have it. He was going to kill the young woman in his own living room. As the kommissar studied her photo, he suddenly realized why. It was uncanny how much she resembled Marlene Eichler. Killing Amanda would feel like killing Marlene all over again. Grutzmacher had to warn her immediately!

He grabbed the phone. His mind raced as he rang Amanda's home number. There was no answer. It was too late for her to be at the gallery, but he'd give it a try. "You have reached the Lee Eichler Gallery. Our hours are from—"

He slammed down the phone.

What was the name of her assistant, Rolf something? Rolf Röhr! He called information. "There is no listing for that name," was the reply. How could the man not have a phone? Then he remembered from routine questioning that Rolf had a room in the home of a widow. Of course—he used her phone. The number had to be in their early reports on Marlene's death. He sat at Rudolf's desk, turned on the computer, and entered the case code.

☙☙☙

Adrenaline raced through Amanda's veins. She had to get out. She turned to the left. A heavy chair blocked her way. To the right was a large table with a brass container of flowers. Reflected in the brass, she could see the dark shape of a man directly behind her. She was trapped. Now she understood why the painting had been placed in this corner.

"Do not try to escape or resist in any way. It will only make things harder for you." The voice was high pitched and mechanical, just as Marlene had described her anonymous caller. She felt a slight movement behind her, then a brush of silk. She looked down. A black silk garment had been draped over her shoulder. The label read *Chanel*. "Put it on. I'm sure it will be most becoming."

"I don't know who you are. I won't be able to identify you. Please let me go. Don't do this."

"Put it on," the mechanical voice repeated.

Slowly she slipped off her sweater, slacks, and stockings, trying to stall until Wolf came home. She began to tremble. "Take off everything, so that you are only wearing the dress, just like in the painting."

She removed her lingerie, put on the dress, and started to turn around.

"Not yet. Close your eyes, and don't open them till I say so."

He was close behind her. She could feel the slickness of latex gloves on her bare shoulders as she was guided toward the straight-backed chair.

"Sit down please."

He pushed her into the chair, pulled her arms behind it, and tied her wrists with some kind of fabric. It felt like one of her nylon stockings. *Where is Wolf? He should be here by now.*

"Open your eyes."

A man stood in front of her wearing a black jumpsuit, surgical gloves, and a black ski mask. There was some kind of metal device over his mouth to change his voice. The eyes staring at her through the slits in the ski mask were icy blue, like those of the man who had attacked her in the parking lot. He walked back to the painting and compared it with the real scene, obviously in no hurry.

༼ၐ༽

He was almost overwhelmed by the sudden desire to smash in her lovely face. But he had to control that urge to enjoy the much more satisfying pleasure of watching her anguish as he destroyed her bit by bit.

Over the years, he had rid the world of many of her kind. He thought back to his first kill, a pretty little neighbor girl who wouldn't give him the time of day. First, he killed her kitten and left it on her swing set. He watched from his upstairs window as she screamed and went flying into her house. Her parents called the police, who questioned him and his mother, among others. He was so convincing in his innocence, he even surprised himself.

A week or so later, his mother went to lunch with friends. The girl came out of her house while he played outside. He told her he found a stray kitten. She could have it if she liked. It was in his basement. When she got to the top of the stairs, he gave her a shove, and she landed hard on the cement floor. When she awoke, she was tied to a chair. He mutilated her with a kitchen knife. Afterward, he put her small body into a plastic bag and buried it under the back porch to hide the evidence of freshly dug ground.

He'd cleaned up the blood and was playing with his train set when his mother came home. The police came again asking if anyone had seen the missing girl. Of course, no one suspected a well-mannered boy of twelve. They thought she had been taken by a pedophile.

He became addicted to the beauty he was compelled to destroy. He felt that he performed an invaluable service getting rid of these human leeches who tempted men, then sucked them dry.

He looked at Amanda. She would try to fight it at first, hoping against hope that somehow she'd be saved. Little by little, with each cut of his blade, she would come to grips with her own mortality. Before long, she would lose hope altogether and begin to die, first on the inside, then after an hour or two, when he had recreated the painting, he would enjoy the magic moment when the light would go out of her eyes.

ღჿღ

"You killed Marlene Eichler." Amanda's voice was strained with fear. "Who are you? Why are you doing this?"

"All in good time," he said.

"You killed Marlene Eichler," she said, "and commissioned Kruger to do the painting of her."

"So I did. And this one of you—his last artistic effort. Unfortunately, he could not go on living. It was just a matter of time until he got stoned and betrayed me."

Amanda continued, stalling for time. Wolf would come home soon, she was sure of it. "Why do the paintings at all?"

The mechanical voice was deadly serious. "To remind the world of the good I've done and to send a warning to women like you." He went over to the desk and picked up an antique knife.

Amanda recognized the curved blade and ivory handle. "I thought the police had that."

"They have one, part of a set of two." He ran his gloved fingers back and forth over the shiny blade.

Amanda's breath became ragged, and the hammering of her heart against her breastbone seemed so loud she was sure that he could hear it. She pulled against the stocking binding her hands.

"It's useless to struggle. You can do nothing. You'll die like just like Marlene, another sobbing, cowardly victim. You're all alike."

"You're the coward. Hiding behind that mask and a false voice—a twisted beast who preys on women."

He approached her and ran the flat side of the knife slowly along her arms and over each breast. Then he took the curved tip and pulled it across her right thigh cutting into the flesh. A thin line of blood sprang to the surface.

Amanda watched the blood run in tiny rivulets down the sides of her leg onto the chair and fall in crimson drops onto the polished floor. "Since you are going to kill me, I think I have a right to know—"

"Rights? You have no rights."

She looked straight into the unnaturally bright eyes. They reflected the red flames of the fire, taking on an eerie glow. Unexpectedly, he turned and walked back to the window and looked out at the velvet night. He stood very still and listened. The shadow of a naked tree limb undulated across the glass to the soft whistling of the wind. He reached up and pulled a cord, snapping the draperies shut.

Amanda's throat became clogged with terror. Her hands were numb from lack of circulation. She wiggled her fingers, and her bracelet with the unicorn made a small tinkling noise. She felt for its pointed little horn and began to pick at her bindings.

❧❧❧

"She's away for the weekend, Herr Kommissar. She'll be back in the gallery on Monday," Rolf said.

"It can't wait till Monday. For her own good, I need to know her exact whereabouts. Now!"

"Well, I'm not supposed to tell. Uh…since it's you, I guess it's okay. She's the guest of Herr Eichler in the Oberkassel section of Düsseldorf. I don't know the phone number or the exact address. I—"

"Never mind. I'll find it." Quickly, Grutzmacher dialed the operator and asked her to connect him with Herr

Wolf Eichler of Düsseldorf. The phone rang and rang. There was no answer.

ৎৎৎ

The sound of the phone startled both Amanda and her tormentor. Its shrill sound pierced the room over and over again. He grabbed the cord and yanked it from the wall. A long silence followed. Once more, she became the focus of those eyes as he started toward her.

CHAPTER 26

Grutzmacher hurriedly put in a call to the Düsseldorf police, and Unter Kommissar Jost answered. "This is Grutzmacher of the Cologne police. I need you to send a car immediately to the Wolf Eichler residence. I have reason to believe a young woman is about to be murdered. I'm on my way there right now."

"We had a riot in the Altstadt and sent all available men there. I'll see what I can do," he lied.

Grutzmacher hurried to his Mercedes and headed out of town. How could Rudolf have been so callous? Hard to believe even he would do such a thing. Heavy fog enveloped Grutzmacher's car, making it hard to see the road. He feared the slightest delay could prove fatal for Amanda.

తారా

Jost would wait to send a car to Eichler's. This was to be Rudolf's big arrest—the one that would get him promoted. Jost would try to get hold of Rudolf before calling for a squad car so that his friend could get there before Grutzmacher.

⁕⁕⁕

The dark figure loomed over her. The knife blade reflected the hearth, and the fire appeared to dance along its edge. Was this it? No! Wolf would come soon. He had to. There was something horribly familiar about those eyes. But since she couldn't see his face or hear his real voice, it was impossible to identify him. She continued to rapidly pick at her bindings.

"I'm afraid your death is going to be slow and painful."

She squeezed her eyes tight against mutilation. Pain shot through the top of her left leg. Amanda opened her eyes. She felt paralyzing fear as she looked down at the blood oozing from twin wounds.

He walked to the liquor cabinet and poured himself a brandy as if he owned the place. "Sorry I can't offer you one," he said. "I'm sure you could use it about now." He studied the painting carefully, then looked at Amanda. "The next cut should be above the left breast, a little deeper this time."

A loud crashing of glass came from the kitchen. He

stopped cold and listened. No sound followed. Slowly he headed toward the kitchen.

Could it be Wolf? Amanda thought. *He'd realized someone was in the house and decided to enter through the back. Thank God he'd gotten here in time.* The electricity of renewed hope buzzed through her body.

The killer entered the kitchen with knife raised.

"Wolf look out!" Her voice sounded dry and shrill.

Fear for Wolf replaced her hope of rescue. Intense banging came from the direction of the walk-in pantry. She heard locks on the backdoor click off and on. A moment later, heavy footsteps ran down to the wine cellar. They seemed to fall on her heart, leaving bruised imprints. Wolf would be okay. He was hiding, waiting for the right moment to attack this monster. What was happening? Another crash shattered the air. He must have overpowered the killer.

"Wolf! Wolf, I'm in here."

Moments later, the killer strode back into the study. He held little Regen in one hand, the knife in the other. "Your rescuer."

She'd forgotten that she put the little cat in the kitchen. Regen's amber eyes were wild with fear. She struggled in the chair, sliding forward a couple of feet. "Leave him alone, you sick bastard!"

She tried to kick him, but he jumped back, laughing, causing the mechanical device over his mouth to emit a high-pitched squawk. It terrified Regen, who dug his claws through the latex gloves and into the hand of his captor, drawing blood. Surprised, the killer cursed and dropped the cat. It scampered out of the study into the hall. He ran after Regen, yelling and thrashing around, knocking over the lamp and table.

Amanda's eyes stung with hot tears as all faith began to drain from her spirit. Wolf would not make it in time. She could not save herself. She could not even save Regen. She felt as if she were passing through a series of shadowy doorways leading closer and closer to oblivion. Then a spark of fury started to burn in her stomach until she was consumed by rage. She could not let him win. With her last burst of strength, she pulled hard against the frayed nylon binding.

The noise in the hallway stopped abruptly. Had he found Regen? *Oh, please God, no*. She looked up as he entered the room.

"That little hell cat can wait till after the main event," he said, walking toward her.

Imperceptibly, Amanda pulled her left hand free of the tattered stocking. She could smell the sweat emanating from his body as he positioned himself in front of her.

Hissing like a coiled snake, the fire burned through a piece of green wood. She jerked her knees to her chest and kicked him in the groin with all of her might. He fell back howling in pain, and his head hit the coffee table with a loud thud. She ran from the study into the hallway.

She heard him let loose a string of obscenities as she

reached the front door. "You'll be sorry, you little bitch."

The door was double bolted. She had just managed to slide back one of the bolts, when he charged through the French doors into the hall. He lunged forward with the knife in his hand. Amanda grabbed a large umbrella stand and hurled it, hitting him directly in the chest.

"I'll cut your heart out for this," he yelled, making inhuman sounds.

She tore open the door and ran out into the night. Her bare feet slipped on the icy walkway as she raced toward her car. She jumped in and banged down the lock just as he pulled on the door handle. Feeling for the car keys, she realized they were in her purse back in the house. Her heartbeat thundered in her ears. She remembered the new car phone and dialed the police emergency number. "A man is trying to kill me!"

The masked face pushed against the glass. He tugged on the handle with all of his strength, but it refused to budge. He ran back into the house.

Amanda screamed Wolf's address into the phone. "Hurry! Please hurry."

She jumped as she heard something smash hard into the windshield. When she looked up, he was back, standing over the hood of the car with a poker. He'd bashed the windshield with such force the glass cracked into long jagged lines.

Amanda leaned on the horn. She pushed in the cigarette lighter. He swung the poker again. With his second attempt, she was covered in shattered glass. He climbed over the hood and started crawling through the broken windshield. The cigarette lighter popped out. She grabbed it and jammed the hot lighter into the mask near his ear. There was a sizzle and the smell of burning cloth and flesh.

"Bitch!" The mechanical voice had reached a new intensity.

She opened the car door to get away, but he was too quick. His hands encircled her throat, trying to crush her windpipe. Running her hand along the seat, she located the car phone receiver and hit him in the temple as hard as she could. He released his grip. Amanda shoved him off herself, escaped the car, and ran.

Two bright headlights turned into the drive. The car lurched to a stop, and the door flew open.

"Amanda?"

It was Wolf. A flood of relief washed over her as she ran toward him.

Another car roared up the driveway, gravel flying as it came to an abrupt halt. Grutzmacher jumped out yelling, "Halt—don't go near her." His gun was pointed at Wolf.

"No, no!" Amanda said. "He's in my car."

Grutzmacher ran over to the Porsche as her attacker was getting out. "Take off that mask. Now. Or I'll shoot."

Slowly, the man pulled off his mask and stood there battered and bleeding.

"Oh my God. It's Rudolf."

The Düsseldorf police arrived. The officers, with guns drawn, walked over to Grutzmacher and Rudolf.

"Lock him up," Grutzmacher said.

Amanda began to shake uncontrollably. Wolf took off his coat and wrapped it around her. "I think she's in shock," Wolf said to Grutzmacher. "She's bleeding. We have to get her to an emergency room right away."

"We'll take my car," Grutzmacher said.

ↄↄↄ

Amanda was given a tranquilizer and treated for the wounds on her legs and small cuts on her feet. "Her physical wounds are mostly superficial, but I'd like her to stay here overnight for observation," the doctor said.

Amanda clung to Eichler. "No, I want to be with Wolf."

He looked at the doctor. "Is that all right?"

The doctor nodded.

ↄↄↄ

In the car on the way back, Amanda told them what had transpired that evening, including about the death painting.

"If you don't mind," Grutzmacher said, "I'd like to pick up that painting tonight. I would request that you stay out of the study until forensics can go over the room tomorrow morning."

Once inside the house, the old policeman walked over to the death painting and shook his head.

"Perhaps I am too old for this job." He showed Amanda and Wolf the two pictures smudged with paint. "Obviously, they were used to create this horrid thing. The one of Marlene Eichler must have been done in a similar way. I am sorry you've been put through so much." He picked up the canvas. "You will both need to come down to my office in a day or two and clear up a few details."

When Grutzmacher was gone, a small black cat ventured out of the hall closet.

"My baby is safe," Amanda said, picking him up and stroking his soft fur.

☙❧

Wolf took Amanda's hand and led her up the stairs. He helped her undress and get into bed, careful not to disturb her bandages. Amanda snuggled close to him, comforted by his warmth, the strength of his arms, the tenderness of his touch.

She knew his love was real. She thanked God for letting her live to experience his greatest blessing of all.

The End

About the Author

P. D. Halt left her native Virginia for New York when she was twenty-one, where she joined the mad men of advertising. She wrote award-winning campaigns, including "Nothing Beats a Great Pair of L'eggs," and shot commercials in Paris for Yves Saint Laurent. Interpublic noticed her, and she found herself living and working in artsy, trendy Düsseldorf, Germany. This led to life changing experiences and the plot for her debut thriller, *When Death Imitates Art*. Halt lives in New York City and is a member of Mystery Writers of America and International Thriller Writers.

CPSIA information can be obtained
at www.ICGtesting.com
Printed in the USA
LVHW011501111020
668522LV00008B/252